Adam Ye

I0616479

Distant Worlds

The Unknown Biomes

To Max, *the* owl.　　　-A.Y.

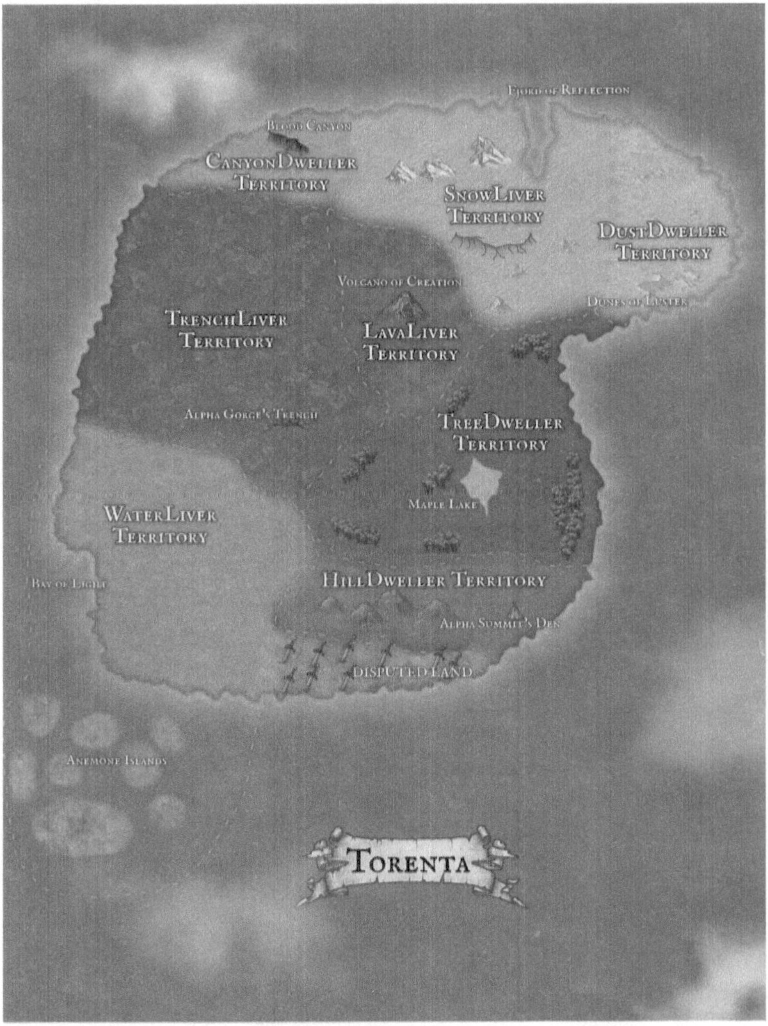
Fjord of Reflection
Blood Canyon
CanyonDweller Territory
SnowLiver Territory
DustDweller Territory
Volcano of Creation
Dunes of Luster
TrenchLiver Territory
LavaLiver Territory
Alpha Gorge's Trench
TreeDweller Territory
Maple Lake
WaterLiver Territory
Bay of Light
HillDweller Territory
Alpha Summit's Den
Disputed Land
Anemone Islands
Torenta

Book Two

Prologue

One Year Ago...

It was a sunny day at the Four-Tribe Academy. There were fish swimming in the stream nearby, the tall grass was waving, and the pups were playing with each other.

Thundergiver and Tempest had other plans, though.

They decided to get away from the other pups and head to the history den and maybe borrow a few tablets from the Head Wolf of the academy, Alpine. They knew that they shouldn't be going there because of the other pups' warnings, but they were just bored and Tempest was complaining that it was "too sunny" for her.

"So, what should we do in the history den?" Thundergiver asked.

"What do you think is a mystery that is interesting and is still unsolved?" Tempest said.

"Well, perhaps if there was a ninth tri–"

"You mean the ShadowCasters," she interrupted.

The two walked in silence for a while. Later, Thundergiver's eyes brightened.

"We could go there to find some clues on where they went," he offered.

"Yes, I agree, but they're wiped out," Tempest countered. "So why wonder about it when everyone knows that the ShadowCasters are gone?"

"Ugh, you're right," he admitted. "Your twenty million points are literally *impossible* to prove wrong."

A moment later, Thundergiver and Tempest arrived at the history den. There was an old birch sign that said History Den. Other than the sign, there was no other object signifying the den's entrance.

The pups entered the den. It was just slightly bigger than the other eight learning dens because it had to accommodate five massive maps and extra history tablets. The den was gloomy; eight old but relatively large candles were the only source of light.

"Alpine said that there would be a sixth map displayed around next week," Thundergiver said, "but I only counted five."

"You mean the one he said was the oldest map here?" Tempest asked.

"Yes, and the one without the HillDwellers on it for some reason."

"That's supposed to be in three months, Alpine delayed the arrival date," she informed Thundergiver.

"Oh well," he said, "let's start trying to look for clues."

Tempest started observing the oldest map, and Thundergiver started droning over tablets to see if there were any relevant topics on the ShadowCasters. The pups searched for twenty minutes and found nothing. They eventually decided to quit.

While leaving the den to go outside, Tempest spotted Alpine. She waved Thundergiver over to try and get some answers.

"Hey, Alpine," Tempest said, as nonchalantly as possible.

"Oh, it's you and Thundergiver," he replied, "why aren't you two outside with the other pups?"

"We tried to find some answers for the mystery of what happened to the ShadowCasters in the history den and came up empty," Thundergiver told him, "so we were wondering if we could find some clues in the library?"

"Of course," Alpine said, "I have seven tablets on the ShadowCasters in general, and I assume a few of them could have some answers. They're in row H, on the third shelf in the history section."

Thundergiver and Tempest thanked him and made a left turn, another left turn, and one to the right. Tempest followed the Head Wolf's instructions and found the tablets within the first fifty seconds of them stepping into the library.

"We're in luck," she said, "as I found one tablet titled, 'what happened to the ShadowCasters?'"

"Let's read it before we're supposed to go to our next class," said Thundergiver.

You may have heard about the ShadowCasters. They were the first tribe to inhabit Torenta nine thousand years ago. The tribe was then allegedly wiped out around eight to seven millennia later. Since then, wolves have tried to answer the question: What happened to the Shadows, and if they still exist, where are they now?

The famous Northeast Mist was the first suspect wolves went to. Lazurite, a LavaLiver explorer, set out to find where the tribe went. He went into the mist and never returned. Around two years after his disappearance, the fog cleared up revealing nothing.

Then, wolves went to the caves of the Anemone Islands. The Anemone Archipelago has been the home of many mysteries, and wolves thought that the islands could house this one, too. Every single secret, solved or unsolved, was always on the ground. No one went into the caves embedded into the cliffs of some of the islands. After the mystery got around Torenta, cave divers went into caves as an attempt to solve it. They came out after expeditions saying that they "just found stalactites and stalagmites."

Although the mystery of the ShadowCasters isn't that popular anymore, some wolves still want to investigate. The best present-day theory is that they are hiding in the newer Northwest Mist on a separate continent called Torento.

"At least we got *some* ideas," Tempest said, "but I don't want to visualize me being a cave diver."

"The Northwest Mist on a separate continent called Torento," Thundergiver quoted, "I wonder if we can go there..."

Part One

The Land of The Two Bird Tribes

Chapter 1

Tempest was unsure about going into the Northwest Mist.

She was also unsure about the fact that she was following a talking gray owl and five other pups who had been kidnapped by some of the alphas of the tribes of Torenta.

"Thundergiver, are you sure about doing this?" she asked. Tempest couldn't find Thundergiver because of the thick fog of the Mist, so she just talked to the air on her left.

"I'm behind you, by the way," the TrenchLiver said, "and I kind of want to see what lies behind here."

Finally turning behind, Tempest countered, "but I don't want to end up like Lazurite!"

"Lazurite was all alone when he went into the Northeast Mist, and guess what? You have five other pups with you, and I'm not sure why, but an owl," Thundergiver told her.

"Well, *if* you don't want to be alone, let's keep pushing," Scoria said. Scoria was the pup of the alpha of the LavaLivers, Coulee. She joined the other pups in the unsuccessful quest of finding the Stone of Tranquility, a stone rumored to grant the six pups that find it Pymarto, or magic, powers and eternal peace to the entire continent.

The owl, Umbra, was flapping his wings wildly yet trying to let the pups follow him.

"Hey, wolves, hurry up!" he said. "We're almost there!"

Instead, it took four hours.

Umbra said the fastest he went from Torenta to his home was just forty-five minutes. Obsidian, another pup in the group, made an excuse saying that he never got out of his hut for more than half of his life and just came across the other pups and followed them here.

At the three and a half hour mark, the pups wanted to give up. Their legs were aching, Frostgem, the sixth member of the group said he hadn't eaten in a day. Scoria told Umbra that he was lying and ate three iguanas right before they met Umbra.

Finally, after nearly three hours and forty-five minutes, the group reached what Umbra called "their destination." Their "destination" was a black expanse of different seven to nine foot mounds. There were only two that towered above the rest. Each mound was hollow, with an entrance made out of wood. They were like polar bears in DustDweller territory.

"Why are there mounds here in the middle of nowhere?" Obsidian asked.

"This complex is made up of fifty mounds," said Umbra, "forty-eight of them act as homes for the owls that work here at the two larger mounds. Each mound fits two owls and their families. Altogether, this complex is called 'customs.' Never heard of it?"

Obsidian shook his head. "I mean, we don't have anything remotely close to this back in Torenta."

"Except for military camps," Solar added.

As Umbra led the pups to one of the larger mounds, murmurs sprang all over customs. "We have visitors!" "We finally have work to do!" "Did wolves really have to come here?" "I was having a good week up until this point!"

The pups were not liking most of the things they were hearing. Tempest's anxiety issues were kicking in, and Frostgem was surprised that his mind-reading, which works on other wolves, wasn't picking up on the thoughts of the owls.

"Well, I guess we're here," Umbra said. "Welcome to customs. We call this customs building A, if you're wondering. Head to the left, please."

The customs building A was very drab. The architects building the mound obviously wanted it to be as cozy as possible, but failed miserably. There were worms squirming all over the ground, the only lighting in there was relatively frightening torches and the walls were just straight dirt.

After turning left, there were four large signs hanging from the ceiling: Newcomers, Owls, Customs Workers, and FVFOL (Frequent Visitors From Outside Lands). Below each sign was a hallway with a few lights coming from the "Newcomers" hallway.

"All right wolves, follow me; we're heading to the 'Newcomers' hallway."

The light from the hallway was actually coming from a large cage. In that large cage was a torch, a branch, and an owl perched on the branch. The owl, which looked like Umbra, spoke to him.

"Toretageö inkolvent rindeßbing!" Said Perched Owl, "nekopek taugan ewemalgł lanþr?"

"Ulmagî caœ kexaö!" Replied Umbra.

"Kilegoot Emersė wanŋ ylentaxat, tilenǧer hulīgæ."

Perched Owl opened a part of the cage to let Umbra pass through and enter the "Owls" hallway.

"Ah, so we have wolves, after so long," said Perched Owl. "One by one, state your name and province of your continent, then your continent."

Solar went first. "Solar of the DustDwellers, Torenta."

Tempest went next. "Tempest of the Water-Livers, Torenta."

"Thundergiver of the TrenchLivers, Torenta."

"Scoria of the LavaLivers, Torenta."

"Frostgem of the SnowLivers, Torenta."

"Obsidian of the LavaLivers, Torenta."

Perched Owl nodded. "I see, you are all from Torenta, we have one WaterLiver, one DustDweller, one SnowLiver, one TrenchLiver, and two LavaLivers. Is that correct?"

"Yes," they all said.

"Now, you will be heading to a debriefing room where an owl will discuss what expectations we have as a tribe in The Land of The Two Bird Tribes."

After walking in darkness for thirty seconds, the pups reached a chamber that looked like a more compact version of the main chamber in customs building A. Facing them was an owl also perched on a branch.

"Greetings, Torentans," the owl said, "you are the first visitors and first wolves to bring yourselves here in hundreds of years. Please keep your attention to me while I give you a debrief of the expectations we have here in The Land of The Two Bird Tribes.

"Welcome to Kloma, or The Land of The Two Bird Tribes. On Kloma dwell two owl tribes: the ShadowBirds, and the MeadowBirds. There is also a MeadowBird separatist group called the Republic of Pŏntibiał Norūeang–the RPN for short–that either want autonomy within MeadowBird territory or full sovereignty from the MeadowBirds; however, they are not recognized by either Kloman Tribes. ShadowBirds are the owls that look like me, or the scout that you came with, Umbra. The MeadowBirds come in a variety of colors, but we have more things to discuss.

"Each sovereign Kloman tribe has a chief, or in Torentan terms, an alpha. You should treat them with utmost respect, as they worked hard to achieve their position as Head of the Tribe. There is also a Head of Kloma, who is referred to as the Hok. If you so happen to meet the Hok, you can address them in two different ways: 'your Hok,' or 'Hok' and then their name. The Hok should also be treated with respect.

"We have three officially recognized languages in Kloma. One language is Jokořinë, the language most ShadowBirds speak, and Morßtïnårow, the language the majority of MeadowBirds speak. The final one is a language called Ipsæk, which all Kloman owls should know. Ipsæk is a co-official language for both tribes, along with their respective languages. Fortunately, although not official between the Shadows, Meadows, or even

Norūeangeans, most owls should know your language that you wolves speak.

"There is a universal currency system that involves minerals called Terön in Jokořinë, Pinł in Morßtïnårow, and Norcot in Ipsæk. The RPN does accept Norcot, but they have another currency system that I won't mention right now. As I've said before, Norcot uses minerals, with copper being the least expensive and garnet being the most. You can get some Norcot minerals in customs building B if you'd like.

"That sums up our debrief today. Now, you will go to customs building B for a 'power check.'"

"What's a power check?" Frostgem asked.

"We're just checking to see if you possess any powers that we should...be aware of," the owl replied. "To your right, wolves."

Once the pups reached yet another chamber, they were greeted by Umbra, who explained what they should do in this chamber.

"Stay single-file," he informed them. "When Dusk here calls your name and tribe, step right in front of the cage so she can do a power scan."

"Thundergiver of the TrenchLivers, please stand in front of this cage," Dusk said.

Thundergiver could feel like he was weightless for a brief five seconds, but in reality, his paws were still on the ground.

"No big concerns," Dusk announced. "Obsidian of the LavaLivers, please stand in front of this cage."

Obsidian went through the same "weightlessness" phase.

"Okay, so he's a Torentan Pymarto. Huh. Frostgem of the SnowLivers, please stand in front of this cage.

"So now we have telepathy; sure. Solar of the DustDwellers, please stand in front of this cage.

"Nothing big. Scoria of the LavaLivers, please stand in front of this cage.

"I see the power of prophecy here. And finally...Tempest of the WaterLivers, please stand in front of this cage.

"Tempest has something; wait a minute..."

"Anything wrong, Dusk?" Umbra asked.

"It's just that...Tempest here has chronoception."

"We need to take her to the chief immediately! Wolves, follow me."

As they followed Umbra, there was light coming from the north side of the building. They reached the light when suddenly they were swarmed by owls.

"It's fine, wolves," Umbra told them. "Anyway, welcome to Kloma."

Chapter 2

Kloma was a lot more disappointing than the pups had hoped for.

This was especially disappointing to Thundergiver, as it was basically a clone of TrenchLiver territory with a lot of owls and no trenches.

"Weren't you saying that you were going to bring us to the chief?" Tempest asked Umbra.

"Oh, now I remember," he said. "Let's head north to Chief Nightfall's compound."

The group walked for half an hour and the pups were entertained by the owls asking them questions in Jokořinë and Ipsæk.

After half an hour, Umbra announced, "we're here. By the way, does anyone speak Ipsæk or is from the bloodline of an alpha?"

"I speak Ipsæk, though not fluently," Tempest replied.

"You never told me that you could speak another language," Thundergiver said.

"I know how to speak *five* other languages," she clarified.

"Okay, but now is anyone from the bloodline of an alpha?" Umbra asked.

"My mother is the alpha of the LavaLivers," Scoria said, "and no way that this is your chief's compound."

Chief Nightfall's compound was almost three times as big as the compound Alpha Sandstone—the alpha of the DustDwellers—lived in, and it made Alpha Coulee's look like an ant. It looked like a beehive and it seemed like it was made of a more "premium" type of dirt. Flying near the grand entrance of the compound were four armored owls.

"What brings you here, Umbra?" One of the owls asked.

"Ah, I knew you were going to ask that, it's for a diplomatic mission," he informed them.

"That would have been a credible way to get in here, but I see wolves next to you."

"This LavaLiver here is the pup of the alpha of her tribe."

"Yes, but why the alpha's pup and not the alpha themselves?"

"Because the alpha is discussing terms with the other alphas on their own continent," Umbra lied.

"Very well," the owl said, "I suppose you could meet Chief Nightfall. But only you and her."

"What?" The other five pups asked.

"Our alphas also sent us on diplomatic missions," Solar told the owl. "Our parents are advisers to them, but we ourselves aren't related to them."

"I know you wolves are lying," the owl said sternly. "Why are you actually here?"

"Tempest here just has chronoception," Frostgem said.

"You shouldn't have lied to me. But this way, please."

Another guard opened up the door showing a grand hall full of paintings of old ShadowBird chiefs, historical ShadowBird moments, and just the ShadowBird landscape. Because the compound was made for owls and owls only, the architects building the compound didn't really put too much attention to the floor. Every forty steps was a tree sapling stripped of its leaves, which the pups assumed was for either decoration or for owls to rest on.

"Allow me to introduce myself," the owl said, "I'm Umbrage, a fourth-ranked servant and an eighth-ranked guard of Chief Nightfall's compound. As a fourth-ranked servant I make sure that visitors, especially visitors from outside Kloma, are as comfortable as possible here. As an eighth-ranked guard, I usually guard the perimeter of the compound and ask why certain visitors are here."

"How does the ranking system work?" asked Scoria.

"How it works for both is that the owls with higher numbers in their rank do less tedious work, while owls with lower numbers in their rank do more things for the chief."

After some silence, a door with two owls guarding it signaled that they were near Chief Nightfall's nest room.

"Umbrage and Umbra," one of the owls said, "what brings you two here?"

"One of these wolves has chronoception," Umbrage said.

"All right. Past this door."

Chief Nightfall's nest room was not much different than the rest of the compound; there was the same "premium" dirt, there were paintings of the ShadowBird landscape, and the same orange-red torches were lit.

Perched on a leafless tree was Chief Nightfall. He didn't really look any different to any of the other ShadowBirds.

"So I've heard that one of you has chronocep-tion," Chief Nightfall said, "so can that wolf please step forward?"

Tempest, from the back of the group, came forward. "It's me."

"What is your name?" Nightfall asked.

"Tempest of the WaterLivers, Torenta," she replied.

"You must be very proud of yourself, Tempest."

"Uh...sure?"

"Well, if you were an owl living here, then you would be right next to me, as my sixth advisor," Chief Nightfall said, "and now that you're here right now, you could be my sixth."

"Er...Chief Nightfall? Isn't it under Shadow-Bird law that only *owls* can be advisors to the chief?" asked one of his guards.

"Oh. Right," he agreed. "Well, I suppose, Tempest, that I should demote you to scout status."

"But Chief Nightfall, the first ten scouts you appoint *have* to be owls," the same guard said, "and she's a—"

"Tempest's going to be my eleventh scout!" Nightfall interrupted.

"S-sorry, Ch-chief Nightfall," the guard apologized.

"We're getting off-topic," said Nightfall. "Tempest, what other skills do you have?"

"I'm just smart in general." Tempest replied. "Though I can speak Ipsæk, I'm still learning Morßtinårow."

"That's great," he said. "But first, I have to know that you're worthy of your position as a scout."

"How?" She asked.

"Right now there is a conflict between the Republic of Pŏntibiał Norūeang and the MeadowBirds, and the Meadows have asked us ShadowBirds to help. I will send you and the other five wolves into RPN territory. When you locate a yellow-dyed mound that looks like the customs building you entered, I want you to find a way to infiltrate it and find a way to kidnap the RPN chief. His name's Veldt, for context. Send him to Chief Lotus, the chief of the MeadowBirds, and she'll figure out the rest."

"We came to this random continent for no reason and then now we get assigned a mission to kidnap a chief of a separatist group on said continent," Scoria groaned.

"Hey, it's for a good cause," Solar countered.

"Enough, wolves," Nightfall said. "I want you on your way right now. Safe travels."

"Wait!" Thundergiver exclaimed, "can we get Umbra to come with us?"

"Umbra has other things to do around my compound," he answered.

"How about Umbrage?"

"Same reason."

"Okay, but can we get a map?" Frostgem asked. "We also need some Norcot for necessities like food."

"There's some vendors in some of the trees," Chief Nightfall informed them, "and as a sponsor of your mission, I am required to give you 150 Norcots."

"We know that copper is the cheapest form of Norcot and garnet the most expensive," said Obsidian, "but what's in between?"

"This chart should solve your problems." Nightfall flipped what was a lever and a roll of paper fell from a hole in the ceiling.

He unrolled the sheet of paper, showing a chart of all the prices that a mineral held.

Norcot sign: ¤

Coal:0.25¤

Copper:0.50¤

Iron:1¤

Gold:2¤

Silver:5¤

Scarlet:7¤ (not in circulation)

Ruby:10¤

Lapis Lazuli:15¤

Titanium:30¤

Diamond:50¤

Garnet:75¤

"So you're basically giving us two garnet pieces," Frostgem said.

"Yes, that's right," Nightfall said, "and I'm glad you have a pouch to store the minerals."

"Okay...thanks. But doesn't that mean we can only make two transactions that are each worth 75¤?"

"There are plenty of these owls called 'accountant owls.' They can change the amount of minerals you have, but you still have the same amount of Norcots."

"Let's be on our way," Thundergiver said.

"All right, see you wolves later," Chief Nightfall said to them.

The pups left Chief Nightfall's compound via one of the four side doors. Solar located some vendors and an accountant owl.

Frostgem and Tempest went to the accountant owl to get some more minerals, while the other four went to find different food options.

"Wait, you're wolves," the accountant owl realized. "Anyway, how many Norcots do you have and how do you want me to distribute them?"

"150." Frostgem laid the two garnet minerals on the table that was in front of the owl.

"So we want ten coppers, nine coals, three irons, four golds, two silvers, four rubies, three Lapis Lazulis, and one diamond," Tempest told the owl.

The accountant gave Frostgem the amount of minerals Tempest requested. "Thank you, come again," said the accountant.

The two pups found the rest of the group not long after, browsing plenty of food options.

"Frostgem," Thundergiver said, "I thought you might be interested in rats–"

Thundergiver was suddenly interrupted by the putting on of a burlap sack on him. The rest of the group had a sack pulled over them as well.

"To the rest of you, is this what being kidnapped feels like?" Solar asked.

"In some way," Obsidian replied. "Wait, I feel dizzy..."

"Me too..." Scoria agreed.

The next thing the pups knew, they were in a prison cell.

The prison cell looked a lot like most cells the pups have been to. It had the coldness of the SnowLiver cell, the slightly large space of the DustDweller cell, and the security of the WaterLiver cell. For some odd reason, there was a canvas at the entrance of the cell that said, *Long Live the RPN!!* with owls triumphantly standing inside the outline of the tribes' territories.

"Do you know where we are?" Frostgem asked.

Looking at the canvas, Tempest said, "Yes. In fact, we finished step one of our mission: infiltrate the compound."

Solar looked at her in puzzlement. "You mean —"

41

"We're in Chief Veldt's compound."

Chapter 3

"We've officially only been in Kloma for less than four hours and we've already been kidnapped," Frostgem said.

"I've imprisoned multiple wolves in my military career but *I've* never been imprisoned myself," Solar added. "So is this how it feels? Frightening? Distressing? A feeling that you could die at any moment?"

"The first two are definitely correct," Tempest answered, "but because this is my third time being kidnapped, I can't really relate to the last one."

"I'm tired," Obsidian announced, "Tempest, what's the time?"

"My mind's a little vague," she said, but what I believe is that it's around...either half an hour before midnight or two hours after midnight. So yeah, we probably need sleep, as we have a chief to kidnap."

The rest of the night was undisturbed to the pups, but to most MeadowBirds and Norūangeans, their days were just beginning. The thick walls and door kept the Norūangean soldiers' sounds out of the cell, so that the pups could get the sleep they needed.

The first pup who woke up, Scoria, woke quite easily. The walls were doing their thing of blocking outside noise and most of the owls were asleep anyway.

"Are you guys up yet?" she asked.

Tempest was the first to respond. "Yes, though I don't want to."

Eventually, Tempest got up and the two just sat in silence for about fifteen minutes when Thundergiver got up.

"How long have you two been awake for?" he asked them.

"I'm not sure," Scoria said, "maybe fifteen—"

"Sixteen minutes and sixty-seven seconds," Tempest corrected.

"Then that's seventeen minutes and seven seconds," Scoria countered.

"Okay, okay, I get the point," Thundergiver interjected. "I wonder who's up next?"

"Me," Frostgem replied.

"Also me," Obsidian added. "So now we're waiting for Solar, which surprises me."

The group whispered silently until Solar woke up nearly half an hour later.

"What took you so long to wake up?" Scoria asked.

"Sorry," he apologized, "it's just that my body's just used to waking up at this time. Besides, we slept relatively late, so doesn't it make sense to *wake up* relatively late?"

The five pups put this into consideration. "Well, I kind of suppose so," Tempest said. "If you sleep late, your cortisol chemicals and acetylcholine chemicals kick off later."

"Change of topic," said Thundergiver, "if we got the choice to choose the first pup to be interrogated, who would that pup be?"

"It has to be Solar," Frostgem said.

"I think so too," Obsidian agreed, "Solar's the best at deception!"

"Hey!" he snapped.

"Well, I guess Solar's going first in interrogation," Thundergiver announced.

"Okay," Solar said, "that's not fair—"

"Do not resist, wolves," someone said as the cell door opened. "You all are going to interrogation. Stay single file."

As the pups were going behind each other, guards were assigned to them. After things were sorted out, the line started moving.

"Is this how it feels to almost be interrogated?" Solar asked Obsidian, who was behind him.

"Kind of," Obsidian replied, "just without a whole lot of propaganda–"

"You have the right to remain silent," the lead owl said. "Also, there are six guards assigned to each of you, so don't even bother thinking about escaping."

Obsidian was right about the propaganda. They were like the canvas in the pups' cell, only about sixty to ninety times larger. Each of them had the same patriotic message that they want to conquer the MeadowBirds and be a direct competitor of the ShadowBirds.

"Now, as we head to the interrogation room, I will let you choose who goes first," the lead owl told them.

"Then it's Solar," Scoria said, "the DustDweller in front."

"Very well. To your right, please."

Solar was led to the entrance of the interrogation room, which had a sign bearing its name above the entrance.

There's an armoury right next to the interrogation room, Tempest thought, *there must be something there that should be harmless yet classified as a weapon.*

"Frostgem, are you able to sneak into the armoury to your right?" Tempest whispered.

"What for?" He asked.

"I need something harmless in there but is still classified as a weapon," she said, "think of a tranquilizer gun and darts."

"I can try, but I've never done this while being held prisoner by six owls."

"You helped us escape Alpha Hailstone's arena!"

"Yeah, only to be captured by Commander Iceberg."

Tempest groaned. "Just go!"

She opened the armoury door and shoved Frostgem inside.

Inside the armoury there were the same weapons someone could find in Torenta, but only specifically made for owls. Everything was wing-mounted, so that an owl could hold something else with their talons.

The six guards finally noticed that Frostgem was missing.

"Wolf! Have you seen the bluish-white wolf?" a guard asked Tempest.

"Er...he went that way." Tempest pointed to the opposite direction of the prison cell.

"Leader!" A guard called. "We have a perfåşel!"

"All twenty-six Lorş̧ɔc, go find the wolf!" The leader informed the guards. "The ten Tongífa, stay here!"

Twenty-six owls, most of whom were guarding Obsidian, Thundergiver, Scoria, and Tempest, all rushed to find "the bluish-white wolf." The last ten made a square around the pups.

At that same moment Frostgem found a small tranquilizer gun and thirty darts. Suddenly, he burst out of the room and shot the tranq darts at the eleven owls guarding the pups.

"Frostgem! You're...here," said Thundergiver. "Tempest, did you lie to them?"

"Yes," she replied truthfully.

Solar then came out of the room. "Frostgem, why are you holding a Meriâtø-F2 KM with wing-mounts? Now, tranquilize the owls inside the room."

Frostgem proceeded without hesitation; he tranquilized both owls, and one of them was a guard and the other was silhouetted.

"Got them."

"Nice work, Frostgem. We might need them, so how much do you have left?" Scoria asked.

"Well, I tranquilized thirteen owls and I originally had thirty, but one missed..."

"So then we have sixteen darts left, counting the miss," she said.

"Okay, so now we can get to chief Veldt using brute force, so I'll go into the armoury to pick out some weapons for each of you," Solar informed the pups."

It only took Solar about two minutes to get the weapons sorted out. Coming out of the armoury, he had five weapons ranging from high-end cross-bows to simple spears.

Each weapon had its own characteristic. One was a weapon that looked like a rifle, another was a crossbow with tons of strings on it, the third was a medium-sized sword, the fourth was a bow with a wooden scope, and the last one was a normal spear.

"Now, I have some weapons that I believe fit each of you and are used in your tribe," Solar said. "Thundergiver, you get the Osprey-37S. It is a cross-bow used by TrenchLiver special forces teams. It has a short range but the accuracy makes up for it.

"Scoria, you get the Zinc Blade Type 8. It's standard-issue for both the HillDwellers and Lava-Livers.

"As for me, I grabbed one of—if not my fa-vorite—weapon out there, the CanyonDweller Resti-nap-34. It is one of the only and best battle rifles in Torenta.

" Tempest, you have the Flux-23 with a scope. It's something a WaterLiver sniper would want to have, especially with its amazing range for a bow and accuracy.

"Finally, Frostgem, you get the Polambo Type 2, which is the spear. It's standard-issue in all Torentan armies but it was created by a SnowLiver.

"Oh, yeah, Obsidian, I know you have Pymarto powers so I didn't choose a weapon for you. But you can have the tranquilizer gun and darts as a last resort."

"That's some...very good weapon knowledge," Scoria complimented, "but we have all these weapons yet no way to kidnap Chief Veldt?"

"Well, I think I saw what was a burlap sack," Frostgem said. "I'll go back in there to confirm."

Frostgem went back into the armoury with the pups staying outside. At the same time as he went into the room, two guards rounded a corner and noticed the pups.

"They're perfåşels!" One of the guards exclaimed, "go get backup!"

"Obsidian, use your tranquilizer gun!" Thundergiver shouted.

Obsidian grabbed his gun and two darts and fired them. One hit the owl who called for backup, but he missed the other guard getting backup.

After the encounter, the pups were now armed and ready for ambushes. Eventually they got distracted by the ruckus that Frostgem was making inside the armoury.

"I found one!" He said triumphantly as he burst out of the armoury. "No owls anywhere, right? Oh."

Frostgem turned to the corner to see a parliament of nearly thirty RPN soldiers. Although they were only armed with smaller versions of the Polambo Type 2s, there were enough to easily kill the pups.

"I know I use the acronym AATUL, but I don't think it's a relevant time to mention it," he said. "I think the best thing to do here is not to brave the storm, but RUN."

The pups took off running with the owls chasing them. They knew the compound well, so they were closing in confidently on the pups.

"Obsidian, your Pymarto powers are the only thing we can use right now! Go use them!" Tempest instructed.

Obsidian got a flashback from back when he was in Alpha Sandstone's compound escaping a horde of DustDweller soldiers. He used the same technique now by levitating in the air and sweeping his arms left. Then, as the soldiers went left he made *them* levitate, and then the owls were thrown to a wall.

Obsidian joined back with the rest of the pups as they kept fending off owls. Except for Frostgem, each wolf took down at least five owls out of the air.

"We can't do this anymore!" Thundergiver said. "We have to hide somewhere!"

The pups went into the first room they could find and locked themselves inside.

The room was nearly dark, save for a torch. The pups couldn't see much, but what they did see was a nest and an owl sleeping in it.

"Uh...does anyone know where we are?" Obsidian asked.

"I think I saw a sign that said 'nest room' above the door, but I don't know," Tempest replied.

"Then who's that owl?" asked Thundergiver.

"Then we completed step *two* of our mission," Scoria said, "finding Chief Veldt."

Chapter 4

"Who has the sack?" Tempest asked.

"Oh." Frostgem realized that he had forgotten the sack back when they ran from the RPN soldiers. "We need someone to tranquilize him in case I take a little long."

Obsidian got a dart and shot it at Chief Veldt as Frostgem left the room.

Where could the armoury be? Frostgem wondered.

Frostgem, using his experience of spying, sneakily went through hallways, careful not to attract any guards patrolling the compound.

I found the armoury! But it's next to three other *armouries.*

Frostgem went into the first room he noticed and grabbed the first sack he saw. He snuck out of the room and headed back to Veldt's nest room.

"You're back pretty fast," Thundergiver said.

"I found another armoury and grabbed a sack from there," he explained.

"Okay, now that we have one, let's put it over Veldt," Scoria informed Frostgem.

He carefully put the sack over the chief and used the drawstring provided with it to seal it up.

"Solar, how long could a subject be sedated with these darts?" Tempest asked.

"Well, those are Tarmaćpoiň-5s, so I estimate about thirty-five to forty minutes," said Solar.

"So then Obsidian, resedate Chief Veldt every half an hour, just to be safe," Tempest told him.

"I get to do something!" Obsidian exclaimed.

"I think we're done, so arm yourselves and let's get out of here," Thundergiver announced.

The pups, one by one, went out of Veldt's nest room and tried to find an exit. There was enough noise to the point that the same soldiers found them again.

"The same perfåşels!" A guard exclaimed.

"Obsidian, what are you doing?" Scoria asked him.

"Just...making...the Sphere of the Tsunami, that ball of light that blew up a small part of SnowLiver territory," he replied. As he was stating his answer, a bullet from Solar's Restïnap-34 and an arrow from Thundergiver's Osprey-37S almost grazed him.

The pups kept fending for themselves while Obsidian was charging up the Sphere of the Tsunami.

"I've charged it full," Obsidian said. "Throwing it...now."

Obsidian threw the sphere as it traveled faster the farther it went. Almost as quickly as it traveled, the sphere blew up. It even vaporized an arrow from Tempest's Flux-23.

The pups, including Tempest, froze. "Who did that?" she asked.

"Me," Obsidian said. "Also, with that, I got you two things. The first thing I gave you is three minutes, and the second is an exit."

"He's right," Solar agreed, "so let's not waste those minutes Obsidian gave us."

The pups took off toward the exit. Exiting through the large, forty feet hole, they noticed the true size of the parliament. The pups only saw the owls in the front of the group, and there were about forty of them in the front. But in the back, nearly one hundred and fifty owls were behind the front forty, which showed how seriously the RPN takes perfåşels, or escaping prisoners. Most of the owls were just unconscious, but Obsidian decided to tranquilize the five owls that were conscious.

Once the pups were out, they decided to hide in a ditch that had a dugout carved inside it.

"So if Norūeangeans are basically Meadow-Birds that want independence from the other MeadowBirds, how can you distinguish RPN soldiers from actual MeadowBirds?" Frostgem asked.

"Well I noticed that almost all of the RPN soldiers have this blue band on their right wing that has the letters 'ELAS' on them," Tempest told him, "but MeadowBird soldiers also have a band, but it's white and usually on the *left* wing and it has the letters 'OIJON.' Under the OIJON acronym is Olmanïł Iscåręmaŷ Jońt Opepaßbon Norūeang. That just means 'Do Not Let the Norūeangeans Take Over,' and I guess we shouldn't trust anyone without a wingband as well."

"I did not understand *one* bit of what you were ranting about," Frostgem said.

Tempest sighed. "Let me just summarize. Do not trust anyone who looks like a MeadowBird without a wingband or owls with a blue wingband with the letters 'ELAS' on them. Everyone else is fine."

"Oh, *now* I get it," Frostgem said.

"Finally," Tempest mumbled.

After some silence, Obsidian said, "I'm ready for lunch. Tempest, what's the time?"

"Fifty-seven minutes and thirty-one seconds before noon," she replied.

"Found these four cloud beavers in the river to the west," Frostgem interjected, "they only show up in cloudy weather and are already pretty rare, so I decided to spear some for lunch."

The pups dug into the cloud beavers and dumped most of the bones into the same river Frostgem found them in.

"Now that we're all full, how will we get to Chief Lotus?" said Scoria.

"We can use the DustDweller way," Solar offered. "If a small group gets lost, they just go in one direction until they hit the sea or find help."

"Then east," Tempest announced. "On our way to Chief Veldt's compound, right before I got knocked unconscious, I could see a huge dome through the tiny holes in the burlap sack. Since in Kloma the sun sets to the south and the sun was facing left, we were going west. Now, we're going *back*, so that means we're going *east*."

"Geez, I was just trying to randomly pick a direction," Solar said.

"There's always statistics in chance," Tempest countered.

Following Tempest's decision, the pups started to go east. Thundergiver was the first to spot what looked like a mound in the distance.

"I think I see Chief Lotus's mound," said Thundergiver, "or a compound, or since there's vegetation there, a hill?"

"It's either a hill or a compound," someone informed him. "But you'll never get into there unless you pass me."

In front of Thundergiver was a bulky owl with an "ELAS" wingband in front of a fence that looked like it went on endlessly.

"Who are you?" Obsidian asked.

"I can't state my name for political reasons," Bulky Owl replied. "What I *can* tell you is that I'm a border guard and I have to stop anyone going in or out of RPN territory without a reason and proper identification, even if they're not...an owl."

"So you're like a customs guard," Frostgem said.

"They're actually the same thing," Bulky Owl clarified, "well, that's besides the point. I need proper identification."

"We're actually diplomats," Scoria lied. "All of us represent a tribe from our home continent, Torenta, and in Torenta, we don't usually have physical identification, so I guess...let us through?"

"Two things wrong here," Bulky Owl said, "first, there's eight Torentan tribes, not five. And why are there two wolves from what looks like the same tribe?"

"He's from a different tribe, I promise," Scoria replied, "and the other two wolves got injured on the way to Kloma, so they had to turn back."

Bulky Owl groaned. "All right, you're through."

The owls stepped to the side revealing a small hole the pups nonchalantly walked through.

"The customs here are very soft," Thundergiver remarked about a minute later.

"I'm even surprised there's even a custom," Tempest said, "back in Torenta, we could just straight-up walk through territories and nobody would care."

The pups walked for about an hour before stopping at a food vendor selling fried mice and boiled insects. They knew they could stop there because the owls working there had white "OIJON" wingbands and anti-RPN artwork.

After spending half an hour eating mice and insects, the group walked for about fifty minutes more before reaching Chief Lotus's hill. The hill was an owl-made mound triple the size of any hill around it. Despite being perhaps the largest owl-made structure in the MeadowBird territory, it was still smaller than Chief Nightfall's compound.

"State your business, wolves," a guard said as the pups approached the entrance.

"We have Chief Veldt in this sack," Frostgem said truthfully, "Chief Nightfall told us to kidnap the chief and give it to Chief Lotus–"

"We've heard enough about that," another guard sighed. "Let's just search the sack and get it over with."

The guard carefully opened the burlap sack and was puzzled to actually see Veldt inside it.

"Oh!" The guard exclaimed, "they actually *do* have Chief Veldt inside the sack!"

"You're kidding," The first guard said, "Let me check."

The first guard checked the sack and had the same reaction as the second one. "Okay, Chief Lotus is in her nest room as of right now. Take a right, then three lefts and a right."

The second guard opened a door showing the main hall. The main hall was almost no different than the hall in Nightfall's compound, only that the paintings had previous chiefs of the MeadowBirds and the MeadowBird landscape. The decorative trees now actually had leaves on them.

The pups took a right, then three lefts and a right to get to Lotus's nest room.

"Is it me, or are some of the leaves here Ujan-ka leaves?" Thundergiver asked.

"Actually, those are Ujänkol leaves," Tempest informed him, "they grow on the same trees as the Ujankas do but are the more common variant."

"I know that you're already inside Chief Lotus's hill because you have Chief Veldt in a sack," said one of the three guards guarding the entrance to the nest room, "but state your business."

"Wait, how do you know?" Solar asked. "Is there like—"

"Classified," another guard interrupted.

"Oh. We have Chief Veldt in a sack."

The third guard gave a light chuckle. "Very well. Access granted. Enter politely."

"By the way, when he means politely, he means carefully," Scoria whispered, "so don't go like 'we have a triumph, and we gracefully give that triumph to you.' Don't barge into Chief Lotus's nest room; it could alarm her and she could send guards to come after us and that won't be good."

Thundergiver carefully opened the door to see actual Ujanka leaves on the walls as well as portraits of Chief Lotus and her parents.

Chief Lotus was a lot different than the alphas in Torenta. Lotus had greenish-yellow wings with a mix of light blue and some very faint orange. She also had a slightly cheerful demeanor that differed from any other tribe leader the pups had come across. The leader with the closest attitude to Lotus was Alpha Ravine, with a less dark presence but is more oppressive.

Chief Lotus was in her nest, chewing on what looked like a mouse. "So I've heard that you were tasked on a specific mission by Chief Nightfall to kidnap that filthy Chief Veldt."

"Er, yes," Tempest replied.

"And do you have him right now?" She asked.

"He's in this sack, tranquilized," Frostgem said, holding up the sack he had been carrying.

"Chief Nightfall told us to kidnap Veldt and send him to you to do the rest," Scoria added.

"Well, I see that you did exactly what he said. You can hand him over."

Frostgem gave her the sack and Lotus stored it inside her nest.

"That's some excellent work, wolves," Chief Lotus said. "Now, you will do a mission under my name. You will go and capture at least thirty Norūeangean soldiers with the wheelbarrows that have the numbers 6 and 7 at the military fort beside my hill. Turn these soldiers into any temporary or permanent military base, saying 'POWFAL' to any guard near that base's prison cells and they will handle the rest. Use that when coming back to my hill."

"Um, sure," Thundergiver said.

"Your mission starts now."

The pups exited Lotus's nest room going into RPN territory for the second time in a day.

Chapter 5

"Wait, I still don't know why we're here, though," Thundergiver said.

"You mean why we are on a mission assigned by Chief Lotus?" Solar asked.

"That's not what I mean," he replied, "what I mean is why are we in Kloma in the first place?"

The pups tried to process what Thundergiver said. "We were just about to part ways after failing to fulfil the Stone of Tranquility twice," Tempest said, "and this was before this random talking owl shows up out of nowhere and takes us into the Northwest Mist–"

"And I suppose that 'random owl' you were just talking about is me."

The pups turned to where the sound originated and Umbra was the first thing they saw.

"Oh, we-we didn't know you were here," Obsidian stammered.

"Come on," he sighed, "I'm a scout. Or a spy, in this case. I'm supposed to go undercover so that I can retrieve information that could be useful to the ShadowBird higher-ups."

"Anyway, now that you're here, can you actually tell us why you made us come to Kloma?" Tempest asked.

"One of you made that decision on your own will," Umbra said calmly. "I just followed your reply. Then came the chronoception thing, and I was *also* following orders in that scenario as well."

"Okay, you win," Obsidian groaned, "change of topic. Are you also on a mission?"

"Yes," Umbra replied. "I'm supposed to infiltrate Chief Veldt's compound and gather intel on battle plans for a potential offensive."

"Well, we kind of infiltrated the compound," Frostgem said, "and we made a big hole escaping it. Perhaps you could enter the compound using that hole–"

"I need a more nonchalant way to enter," Umbra interrupted, "don't you think that's too obvious?"

"He's right," Scoria nodded. "But other than that, we don't have any advice for you. However, where is the closest military base to Chief Veldt's compound but is still far from the border?"

"Try the Mæsteraüt Permanent Support Base, or the PSB," Umbra said, "are *you* on a mission?"

"We're just trying to hold thirty Norūeangean soldiers prisoner," Thundergiver replied.

"Oh, that's super easy," Umbra scoffed, "just wait for some soldiers outside a big entrance and then make your move."

After some conversation, the group decided that talking too much out in the open would make them easy targets, so the pups said goodbye, went south while Umbra went north.

"You are all under arrest for attempting to cross a closed border," said the border guard that the pups encountered half an hour later.

"We literally came out of RPN territory almost two hours ago," Thundergiver said.

"Actually, it's a one-way border," the guard corrected. "Anyone in RPN territory can exit our territory but anyone trying to get in can't..."

"Was that the wrong time to tranquilize the guard?" Obsidian asked.

"You did good," Scoria assured him, "but it depends on how many darts you have left."

"Six."

"Oh, then that's fine."

"But we need more than thirty to tranquilize thirty soldiers," Tempest countered.

"We don't have to knock them out in one run," said Scoria, "also, we forgot to bring the wheelbarrows."

The pups, all admitting that they forgot to bring the wheelbarrows, headed back to Chief Lotus's hill. They found a building that was relatively large but was still smaller than the compound beside it.

The building, named the Chief Pasture Military Headquarters as shown by the large wooden sign put nearly at the top, was almost like a town built just for the purpose of protecting the compound and everything in its area. The walls were made of large pieces of stone and the two entrances were made of pure limestone, which symbolised patriotism and purity. As what the pups found out later, the base is named after Chief Pasture, the MeadowBird's third chief who created the MeadowBird military, the Norcot currency system, and the Morßtinårow language.

The pups entered the military base after going through yet another "state your business check" by a guard. It took them fifteen minutes to find the wheelbarrow station, and another ten to find an armoury to stack up on ammunition and tranq darts.

Fortunately, when the pups came back to the same place where the border guard was, he was still unconscious. Just to make sure, Tempest quickly poked the guard with a tranquilizer dart, left it there for ten seconds, and took it out.

"Tempest, you should have left it there," Solar told her, "it's pretty much useless at that point because the toxins are either already in the owl's body or got stuck in the feathers."

"I have tranquilizer ink, though," Frostgem offered. "I quickly grabbed it while you guys were getting ammunition."

"So we can just dip the useless dart to make it use*ful*," Tempest said.

Tempest gave the dart to Frostgem who carefully dipped it into a clay container that had an opening that could open and close.

"There, that should do it," said Frostgem. "I could dip some of your arrows into the tranquilizer ink to make them very large tranq darts."

Ten minutes later, one-third of all the arrows the pups got from the base were covered in tranquilizer ink.

"I found our first potential prisoner," Solar informed the group. "Tempest, could you just snipe him from long range?"

"Already knocked out," Tempest replied.

The pups kept tranquilizing RPN soldiers, and this kept on going until about fifteen owls were knocked out.

"Let's grab the soldiers and head to a base," said Solar, "but not before I get this last one."

Borrowing Thundergiver's Osprey-37S, Solar was almost dead on with his shot, but a gust of wind forced the arrow wide, catching the attention of the soldier he was aiming at. Solar didn't hide, so the owl thought that he was the one who shot the arrow.

"Hey, I think I know you," the soldier said.

"You definitely don't know me," Solar replied.

"You're one of the perfåşels!" he realized, "okay, you're under arrest, and bring your other friends out as well..."

"I needed an ego boost," said Obsidian. "Although we should pack up and leave RPN territory ASAP."

It took the pups twelve minutes to locate the tranquilized owls and put them into the wheelbarrows. Then, it took them another half hour to get out of RPN territory.

"Does anyone hear wingbeats?" Thundergiver asked.

"The only owl I see is a ShadowBird, and that's not that big of a concern," Scoria replied.

The pups reached the Mæsteraüt PSB forty minutes later. The Mæsteraüt PSB was just a smaller version of the Chief Pasture base.

"POWFAL," Tempest told a guard near the prison cells.

"Oh, you wolves must be the ones Chief Lotus sent," the guard said. "We'll deal with the rest–"

"WE'RE UNDER ATTACK!!" An owl exclaimed.

"That's a rare occurrence," the guard remarked. "Wolves, follow me to my defending post so that you could help me."

The pups climbed overlapping stairs to get to the guard's defense post. Cell Guard's "post" was a catapult, and beside it were jagged rocks and what looked like large owl-made tumbleweeds.

"When I say 'fireball,' I need one wolf to light the tumbleweeds on fire with the liquid fire starter that's next to them," Cell Guard instructed the group, "then, I need another wolf to quickly carry the tumbleweed on fire to the catapult and place it so that I could launch it.

"When I say 'avalanche,' I need three wolves to bring one of those heavy rocks onto the catapult.

"Finally, I need one wolf to help me bring back the launch rope after every single launch. The launch rope is hooked to a mechanism that releases the rope when a lever is switched, triggering the catapult to make the object inside it fly. That same wolf also helps me adjust the catapult's angle so that we can get as many soldiers taken out as possible."

The pups decided who would do each role. Obsidian and Scoria were in charge of the tumbleweeds, as any accidental burns wouldn't affect their fire-resistant fur. Thundergiver, Solar, and Frostgem were in charge of carrying the boulder to the catapult because they were the strongest. Finally, Tempest would be the catapult angler because everyone thought that she could use her thinking to efficiently angle the catapult.

"I think we need to catapult something," said Cell Guard, "fireball!"

Scoria dipped part of a tumbleweed into the fire starter and handed it over to Obsidian. He threw the flaming tumbleweed onto the catapult while Tempest used the lever to launch the catapult.

The flaming tumbleweed went smack in the middle of a large horde of thirty Norūeangean soldiers. Although about twenty managed to escape the inferno, ten couldn't escape and were badly burned.

Just as the pups were celebrating, a flurry of arrows missed them.

"I forgot to tell you guys to beware of what we like to call 'retaliation arrows'" Cell Guard informed the pups.

Another dozen arrows missed the group.

"I think we should bombard them even more," Solar said, "that way, they don't have a chance to bombard *us*."

"Very well then, let's get two avalanches at a time and a fireball straight ahead!" Cell Guard told the group.

The three boulder carriers carefully loaded a boulder onto the catapult as Tempest was grabbing the launch rope and attaching it to the triggering mechanism. The boulder landed with a loud *thud*, potentially crushing a couple of soldiers with many more fleeing. The boulder carriers did the same thing for the next one.

Meanwhile, Obsidian was giving out some of the group's tumbleweeds to other groups that were running out of them. Scoria was doing the same thing, only with flaming tumbleweeds.

"Obsidian, we need one fireball," Tempest said. "Ask Scoria to prep them while I get the catapult adjusted to $9.35°$."

He nodded before telling Scoria to return to making flaming tumbleweeds for them.

"Yeah, I already did it," Scoria said in response. "If you want to check, it's in the catapult right now."

"How–" Obsidian was cut off by the launching of the flaming tumbleweed that Scoria did indeed put in the catapult.

"Let's stay behind the catapult in case of retaliation arrows," Cell Guard said.

What sounded like the sound of doors coming off came from the ground level. Owls were chanting "ELAS," signaling that RPN soldiers destroyed the doors and were trying to capture the base.

"Does anyone have their weapons?" Frostgem asked.

"I'm afraid we left ours back at the prison cells," Thundergiver replied.

The RPN soldiers split into smaller groups and were trying to find the way to get to the flagpole where the MeadowBird flag of horizontal green, orange, light blue, and yellow stripes and a red cross hung. The pups and Cell Guard decided to guard the

flagpole along with many other MeadowBird soldiers.

The Norūeangean soldiers climbed up and
eventually found the flagpole. They decided to attack
from all directions, leaving the pups helpless.

Chapter 6

"This is one of those times where I don't have any plan," Tempest admitted.

"You *should* have a plan now that the Norūeangeans have our flag," Frostgem said.

Tempest looked to see three MeadowBirds flying away with the MeadowBird flag, replacing it with a black, blue, and green vertically striped flag.

"Wait, Obsidian, levitate up to the RPN flag and burn it using a flaming tumbleweed!" Tempest told Obsidian.

He asked Scoria to give him the biggest tumbleweed in their arsenal, started levitating, made the flag catch fire, and then came back down to the ground like nothing ever happened.

"I hear battle cries, so I presume the RPN soldiers haven't left," Thundergiver observed.

"Obviously," Solar said, "they're trying to capture an entire military base, and of course the MeadowBirds aren't going down without a fight."

"Let's just stay here in case more soldiers try to enter," said Tempest.

After half an hour's worth of "fireball" and "avalanche," the Norūcangeans surrendered and left with their dead and injured comrades. A new MeadowBird flag was hung up in response to the one taken away.

"The Norūeangeans surrendered," Solar confirmed. "Well, I guess we need to be on our way. "

"You and your group are leaving?" Cell Guard asked.

"We imprisoned fifteen soldiers but we need thirty," he replied.

"And after that we need to report to Chief Lotus," Obsidian added.

"Well, thanks for helping me anyway," Cell Guard said.

The pups said their goodbyes to Cell Guard and got weapons and ammunition because their old weapons were either stolen or broken in the battle. The group found a small dugout deep inside the base to sleep because it was getting late. They all agreed that they could get another fifteen soldiers imprisoned during the next day.

The next day, Frostgem woke the pups up by announcing that he had just caught another cloud beaver and two ducks. Nobody listened to him, so he stayed in silence for twenty minutes before the second pup, Thundergiver, woke up. It took another thirty-five minutes for the last four to wake up, and during those twenty minutes, Thundergiver decided to imprison the fifteen soldiers the pups needed to imprison.

"That was some good sleep I got there," Obsidian remarked, "so are we going to get another fifteen soldiers like we did yesterday?"

"I guess," Scoria replied.

"We should go to another spot," Tempest added.

"You don't have to, because fifteen—in fact—sixteen of them are in the cells under POWFAL," Thundergiver interrupted.

"Is that why you were gone?" Solar asked.

"Yes," he replied, "I was kind of bored waiting for you guys to wake up, so I told Frostgem that I was going to get some soldiers within forty-five minutes, and I came back just in time."

"Then we can head back to Chief Lotus's compound!" Obsidian realized.

After eating a twenty-five minute breakfast, the pups walked all the way back to Chief Lotus's hill.

"POWFAL," Tempest said to one of the guards at the entrance of the compound.

"You're them," said a guard. "To Chief Lotus's nest room, please."

The group, still remembering the route to Chief Lotus's nest room, were wondering what mission they would get next, or even if they would even *get* a mission.

"POWFAL," Tempest said again.

The guard beside the door opened it without saying anything.

"The wolves," Chief Lotus said. "I see that you said POWFAL twice to guards at the Mæsteraüt PSB, and each POWFAL contained fifteen Norūeangean soldiers. Well done."

"So do we get another mission?" Solar asked.

"As of right now, *I* don't have any missions for you," she answered, "though I suppose that Chief Nightfall might assign you more things. You're dismissed."

The pups walked out of Lotus's hill and started to walk back to Nightfall's compound.

"Something about the tribe name 'Shadow-Birds' doesn't sit right to me," Tempest told the group about ten minutes later.

"Seems ordinary to me," said Thundergiver.

"Have you heard of the Shadow*Casters*?" she asked, slightly offended.

"Oh, right."

"Not only do they have a similar tribe name, they don't live in their home anymore. And according to myths, the ShadowCasters lived behind the Northeast Mist, and the ShadowBirds live behind the North*west* Mist."

"Then we should ask Chief Nightfall if it's true," said Obsidian.

The pups walked for another half hour, before Solar told a guard near the entrance that they were sent to visit Nightfall under the order of Chief Lotus. Oddly enough, the guard bought it and let them go inside.

Tempest led them to Nightfall's nest as she was the only one who remembered the route.

"We're sure we're going to ask Chief Nightfall about the ShadowCasters," Tempest said.

"Yes," Scoria confirmed.

The pups opened the door to find the same owl who made their first ever mission.

"So I've heard that you not only imprisoned Chief Veldt, but you've also imprisoned several Norūeangean soldiers," said Nightfall.

The pups nodded in agreement.

"I understand that these missions can be tedious, so Chief Lotus and I won't give you any quests for quite a while. Also, Tempest of the WaterLivers, you earned the scout position. In fact, *all* of your friends are scouts as well."

"Wait, are we supposed to be happy or slightly concerned?" Obsidian whispered to Thundergiver.

"One more thing: Tempest, how long has it been since I assigned your first mission?"

"Three days...four hours, one minute, and now eleven seconds," she answered quickly.

"I see, you must be a direct descendant of Void, the creator of the five continents on Ğürsa: Kloma, Torenta, Petasami, Vetasami, and Pymarto, as well as the ruler of Daskīmé," said Nightfall.

"Whoa, slow down," Frostgem told him. "What's this 'five continents' thing? What's Ğürsa? And what do Pymartos have to do with this?"

"Let me answer your questions in order: on the planet that you and I live on, there are five continents dominated by a different animal, and two of those continents are our home continents, Torenta and Kloma. Ğürsa is the name of our planet, and Pymartos are from the continent of Pymarto. It's considered the most sacred continent."

"Good to know," Thundergiver nodded, "but how come we, or even Tempest, don't know about this stuff?"

"It's a long story," Chief Nightfall replied, "but to summarize, Void doesn't like Torenta after what happened to his sibling, who was killed after wolves there didn't like being ruled by them. Void punished them by giving them limited knowledge about Ğürsa."

"Do you know about the Stone of Tranquility?" Tempest asked suddenly.

"We have it in my compound," Nightfall replied. "I can take you there, even giving you the power to fix a war as a reward."

Chief Nightfall led them through a series of hallways with some of them even going underground.

"Are you sure this isn't a trick?" Tempest whispered to Thundergiver.

"Chief Nightfall isn't deceptive like Alpha Atoll," he replied.

After some more walking and flying, the final hallway was a dead end with an isolated room to the right.

"This is the stone room," Nightfall told the pups as he opened the door.

The stone room was a barren room with more of the premium dirt. The only thing that stood there was a stone a little bigger than the fake ones on a granite pillar. The stone, unlike the fake ones, didn't have a glow.

"Is there a war going on in your home continent?" Chief Nightfall asked.

"I think it's called the HillDweller-WaterLiver Fourth Annexation War," said Scoria.

"Okay," the chief nodded. "Oh, the Stone of Tranquility, give peace to all the wolves affected in the HillDweller-WaterLiver Fourth Annexation War!"

The Stone of Tranquility glowed a bright blue, rose from its stand, and then fell back onto it, all within seven seconds.

"Let's hope that the war ended," said Frost-gem.

"I'll lead you back to the top of my compound," Nightfall told the pups, "you guys can even leave Kloma, but that's if you want to."

The chief led the pups back to his nest room. There was one less guard outside the door because the chief was not inside the room.

"Can we come back?" Thundergiver asked.

"You're all welcome back," Nightfall replied, "just make sure to use the FVFOL hallway when passing through customs. Also, *if* you're going back, make sure to use customs building *B*."

"Well, nice knowing you, and, well, all of Kloma," Solar said.

"We'll probably come back soon, but there's this thing called 'homesickness' and we need to make sure it's solved," Obsidian added.

"You've been away from LavaLiver territory for almost two and a half months and you never complained about homesickness," Scoria told him.

The pups waved goodbye to Chief Nightfall and exited the compound. Walking back to the customs they ran into Umbra.

"Going back already?" he asked them.

"Come on, we got two missions assigned by two chiefs, one of them was to kidnap another chief, and for the other one, we were practically serving in the MeadowBird army!" Solar told Umbra, "obviously we had to go back to Torenta to rest."

Umbra nodded in agreement, knowing that the pups had no idea that they were doing missions under the leaders of two tribes.

"Thanks for coming to Kloma, though," he said, "maybe one day, *I* can visit Torenta. That's, if I have spare time, though."

The group laughed and said goodbye to each other. Umbra was going to report to Chief Nightfall to the west while the pups were going to customs to the east.

Fifteen minutes later, the pups were stopped by their first customs guard. The guard was blocking the entrance to customs building B.

"Going back to Torenta?" The guard asked.

"Yes," they all replied.

"Go inside and make a left," he informed them, "thank you for visiting the continent of Kloma."

The pups went inside the customs building and made a left. They found themselves in a similar first chamber from the A building. Nothing or nobody was there to stop them so they exited the building.

The pups made one last look at Kloma, which was just the mounds and the two customs buildings, and then the group started making their journey back home.

Three hours and forty-five minutes later, the group saw their first glimpse of what was Canyon-Dweller territory. They all ran to the light, immediately blinded by the light from the sun because they haven't seen that much sunlight in the past four and a half days.

"Well, I guess we fulfilled the Stone of Tranquility," Thundergiver announced, "as well as going past the Northwest Mist, and discovering an entire continent and two tribes. Well, three, if you count the RPN. As a group, what's there to do?"

"I guess we'll go back to our homes," Solar said. "I'm going back to being a DustDweller soldier, that is, if the leaders haven't kicked me out."

"Me and Thundergiver are going back to the Four-Tribe Academy," Tempest said, "our twenty-day you-can-be-out-of-the-academy time period has expired.

"I'm living solo," Frostgem put in. "I'll probably visit Obsidian every now and then because we both live alone."

"I'll live with my mother, like I've always been," Scoria added.

The pups, for the third time, said goodbye, but this time to each other.

Chapter 7

Before heading back to DustDweller territory, Solar stopped at the last Torentan town he went to: Zodorai. Zodorai is a CanyonDweller town that the pups spent time in right before Umbra showed up.

Solar came across Ravine Square, named after the current CanyonDweller alpha. In Ravine Square were different vendors, but he opted for Ompiar Vetorow plo Tiger, a restaurant that Thundergiver's family owned.

"Table for how many?" a waiter asked Solar.

"One," he replied.

"To table three, please."

Solar walked to table three, pleased to be relaxed for the first time in about a week.

Three minutes later, a waiter came up to him. "Due to supply issues, we only have the eight-in-one meal," she said. "Is that fine with you?"

"I *am* hungry, so yeah."

The waiter walked into the kitchen and gave a cook an order to make the eight-in-one meal.

Twenty minutes later, the cook came out of the kitchen with food stacked on top of each other. "Fine dining from all corners of the continent," the cook said unenthusiastically.

Solar looked at the plate. *They're serving me glop?* he thought. *Even army food looks better than this.*

He reluctantly started poking the food, which got him side-eyes from the other diners. Eventually, he did start eating the meal, but it took him about an hour and ten minutes to finish it.

A waiter came by and asked, "Are you finished?"

"I guess," Solar replied.

"I need two iron nuggets," the waiter told him.

Solar gave the waiter two Norcots that Frostgem gave him when Frostgem was trading with an accountant owl.

"Thank you, come again."

Solar exited plo Tiger, his stomach not feeling great. Looking at a map that was on the west side of the square, he picked up the directions to Alpha Sandstone's compound.

Solar walked for the entire afternoon, from the dry paths of CanyonDweller territory to the frozen landscape of SnowLiver territory, and finally to the hot sands of DustDweller territory.

It was about six hours after high sun when Solar finally saw Alpha Sandstone's compound. He walked in casually, looking to find the sleeping quarters.

It was empty.

That's weird, Solar thought, *there's usually always a division hanging out here. Except for that one time with Obsidian.*

Solar left looking for some place that served food. He ran into Xerocole, a soldier in his division.

"Xerocole! Glad to see you," Solar said. "Where's the rest of the Rattlesnake Division?"

"Disbanded," he replied.

"Really?"

"Yeah. Have you been living under a rock? The war ended."

That must have been us! Solar realized that, *after Chief Nightfall told the Stone of Tranquility to end the WaterLiver-HillDweller war, it did end.*

"What happened to our comrades?" Solar asked.

"Most left, like me. Some, like Woodrat and Badger, became reserves for divisions that are still active. You're actually one of the three soldiers that got released from your military duties, the others being your siblings Caracal and Gecko."

"How?"

"Everybody knows. You've gone AWOL."

"Oh, that," Solar remembered. "I had to leave because I was trying to stop the war! Just being in an army won't help."

"And...you did?" Xerocole asked.

"In a way," he said.

"Well, you're wrong," Xerocole countered. "The alphas met together at Alpha Timber's tree, where Alpha Atoll agreed to give the disputed land back to the HillDwellers. And I'm pretty sure you didn't do anything there, no?"

Solar was desperately trying to find a way to change the subject. "Where's the nearest place to eat?"

"No clue," Xerocole replied.

Solar thought that the conversation was getting nowhere, so he left, still trying to find a place to eat. Knowing that he couldn't eat at any place related to the military, he decided to just hunt, even though the last time he hunted was when he was two. Half an hour later, Solar did manage to hunt a jackrabbit, and he ate it right where it was caught.

Now that I got the food situation solved, how do I fix the shelter problem? Solar wondered. He didn't want to go back into the military sleeping quarters because he would most likely get into trouble, but he didn't like the idea of sleeping on the desert sands alone. Solar kept thinking of ideas, but none of them seemed to be logical. After some thinking, he realized that he could live with his father, Ferret.

That was a great idea until Solar realized that he *forgot* where Ferret lived.

When Solar was about six months old, his mother died as a prisoner-of-war after being caught by WaterLivers as a double agent working for the TrenchLivers. Ferret couldn't handle raising three pups on his own, so he sent Solar's older sister, Caracal, to the DustDweller army, with Solar following two months later. Gecko—Solar's younger brother—stayed with Ferret for about a year, and then got sent to the military, too.

Because Solar left Ferret and his house when he was only eight months old, his memories in the house were very vague, and the area around the house was vague, too. The only thing he could remember about the town as a whole was that its name started with an "L."

Solar remembered that he had the ability to memorize an entire list of soldiers' names in an eighty-soldier division. He also knew the names of every Tree and Dust town and village.

But even if he started searching now, it would take him forever.

That's when Solar realized: he had Pymarto powers.

When Chief Nightfall fulfilled the Stone of Tranquility, it was probably the reason why the war ended. With that, the pups should have gotten Pymarto powers. They didn't fulfill the stone, but at least they were in the presence of it.

Solar then said to himself a random DustDweller town, and strangely, he *was* in that town. He searched the town, seeing if there was anything to him. This kept on going for more than an hour, town after town.

After the eighteenth town, Solar was ready to give up. *There are twenty towns and villages in DustDweller territory, though,* he thought, *and I hope that one of the last two is where Ferret lives.*

So Solar said the second-to-last town, Lesenk, and he was instantly teleported to the town. Lesenk wasn't the largest of towns, but it wasn't the smallest of villages, either. For the first time in an hour, something felt different in him. *Nostalgic,* he thought.

Solar ignored the feeling and started searching the town as normal. He rounded a corner and the nostalgic feeling came back to him. In front of him was a relatively small sandstone house, barely enough to fit a pack of five.

This time Solar couldn't handle the nostalgic feeling. He opened the door to see two wolves, one of whom was Caracal, and the other was who Solar believed was Ferret.

"I'd never been expecting a family reunion for the second time in less than a week," Ferret said.

"Wait, Solar, weren't you also dismissed from your military duties?" Caracal asked Solar.

"Yeah, I went AWOL," he admitted, "I heard you were also released. What for?"

"Our general decided to release the entire division the day the war ended," she replied, "and for whatever reason, he released soldiers early, which technically meant that I was RUSC, Released Under Strategic Circumstances."

"Enough about military talk," said Ferret. "What happened to Gecko? I need an answer out of you."

"He was released quite early," Caracal answered, "though I still don't know why. I think he's now a battle advisor for Alpha Timber, strangely."

Just after Caracal said "strangely," a group of what looked like the same flaming tumbleweeds from Kloma fell from the sky.

"Are we under attack?" Ferret asked.

"We can't be! The war ended only a day ago!" said Caracal.

The fireball kept bombarding Lesenk, perhaps even attacking other DustDweller towns as well.

"Everyone, do not resist," someone called to the town. "We are the WLWAA, the WaterLiver War Arresting Administration."

Ferret shook his head. "There's another war happening."

Thundergiver and Tempest were making the long trek back to the Four-Tribe Academy, all the way in the northwestern tip of HillDweller territory. They ate lunch with Thundergiver's parents, and they said hi to Lionfish, a prisoner formerly under the regime of WaterLiver alpha Atoll. Then, they were sneaking through the safer forests of TreeDweller territory because they still hadn't realized that the Hill-Water War ended. They got to the academy right when the pups of the academy were getting ready to sleep, two and a half hours after sunset.

At the academy, they first wanted to say hi to Alpine, the Head Wolf of the Four-Tribe Academy.

They smelled the earthy odor of the snake-like hallways on the way to his room.

When Thundergiver and Tempest went past the Ujanka entrance leaves, they saw Alpine at his desk, not organizing tablets for the first time. He was visibly stressed, looking through a pile of what looked like letters.

"Uh, is everything all right, Alpine?" Thundergiver asked.

"Can't you see? Obviously not," he replied. "I'm just looking through different letters Timber sent me of different wolves saying that yet *another* war is happening."

"So it's the same exact war?" Tempest asked.

"No, it's the WaterLivers versus everyone, and it apparently started because of... 'six pups triggering the alpha of the WaterLivers, Atoll, who wants revenge on them by attacking their home tribes, plus the CanyonDwellers and the TreeDwellers.'"

"That can't be us, right?" Thundergiver said, shaking his head.

"There are thousands of pups across Torenta, and we're just six out of many," Tempest added.

"Well, you two should get some rest," Alpine told them. "Also, tomorrow, I'm making an announcement that I won't be taking any more requests to leave the academy, just a heads-up."

"Thanks for letting us know," Tempest said.

Tempest and Thundergiver walked through the same snaky hallways that they walked in a few months ago. They passed the library, the same library they checked out a year ago, when they were trying to find where the ShadowCasters were living.

"Why is there still another war going on?" Thundergiver asked Tempest.

"My guess is that Chief Nightfall told the Stone of Tranquility to end *just* the Hill-Water War," she replied, "if he said to end all wars on the entire continent, that would make everything actually better."

Thundergiver took that into consideration, pondering it for the rest of the night.

Chapter 8

Frostgem arrived at his TreeDweller hut at around midnight, nonetheless exhausted from the day.

He spent some time at one of his bunkers he had built in CanyonDweller territory. At around sunset, Frostgem made a detour to a small southeastern TrenchLiver village for some food. The Four-Tribe Academy was less than a mile away from the village, so some pups from the academy came to say hi to the locals.

After filling up on food, Frostgem entered TreeDweller territory, still not knowing that the previous war has ended. *There are way more Water-Livers in Tree territory,* he thought, *the only WaterLivers to step inside it were probably diplomats and Alpha Atoll. Oh, and Tempest.*

When Frostgem arrived at his hut, the first thing he did was to clear the rotting food out of the hut's storage space. When he was going to greet his pet squirrel, he realized that it wasn't there. Frostgem assumed it had escaped while he was with the pups for a couple months. He decided to keep his former pet's living space as is in case he wanted to keep another pet.

Lying down on his fern and moss bed, Frostgem remembered one of his old friends, Leafseed. They spent most of their day with each other, making up stories and playing "guess what I'm thinking about in five seconds" with Frostgem's telepathy. That changed when Leafseed laughed at Frostgem for accepting the offer of going to find the Stone of Tranquility with Thundergiver and Tempest.

The next day, Frostgem did his morning routine: waking up, stocking up on food, checking the exterior of the hut for anything needing repair, and catching some fish at Maple Lake.

When Frostgem was going back to his hut, he saw about forty massive boulders fall from the sky, barreling toward different spots in TreeDweller territory. Frostgem ran back to his hut, but knowing that his hut's roof and the tree above it wouldn't protect him, he instead ran toward the closest town, which just so happened to be the capital of the TreeDwellers.

Frostgem took shelter in the den of someone who was now the closest TreeDweller he knew. The TreeDweller, whose name was Canopy, was puzzled as to why Frostgem was in his den.

"There were boulders falling from the sky when I was at Maple Lake," Frostgem said. "This town, Redwood Village, was the closest town, so I just took shelter here."

"But couldn't you just hide in your hut?" Canopy asked him. "I assume your hut's closer to the lake."

"Okay, that's true," he admitted. "But if my hut gets crushed, no one would notice until three days later—"

Frostgem was cut off by the boulders smashing into the ground. Two were very close to hitting Canopy's den, and some other dens weren't so lucky.

Canopy, surprised that two massive rocks hit the ground right next to his den, checked the exterior. There were about twenty-five boulders scattered around Redwood Village, with more than half of them surrounding Alpha Timber's tree. Fortunately, the tree itself was not harmed.

A few minutes later, Alpha Timber came down from his tree to oversee the damage. He made sure that more TreeDweller soldiers were guarding the outskirts of Redwood Village.

"Everyone remain calm," Timber said. "This is supposed to happen."

"What do you mean?" a TreeDweller asked him. "You're telling us that our town—not to mention the capital of our tribe—getting attacked is 'supposed to happen'?"

"The WaterLivers declared war on us."

The residents of Redwood Village froze and looked at Alpha Timber, and then started going crazy.

TreeDwellers were screaming and running around the town as a dozen more boulders came raining down on them. Some wolves even grabbed their personal defense weapons to join the soldiers guarding Redwood Village's perimeter. In all the chaos, Canopy bailed on Frostgem, taking a spear with him to perhaps join the soldiers.

Frostgem, being the only wolf not doing anything, randomly got a flashback of him getting one of the sacks back in Chief Veldt's compound. Then, he got another flashback of borrowing Tempest's Flux-23 to try to take down some of the RPN soldiers in that big horde.

Those flashbacks gave Frostgem an idea: he could try and infiltrate Timber's tree, grab a weapon and defend the capital with both the residents and the soldiers.

Thankfully, he *had* infiltrated Timber's tree multiple times with Leafseed. In fact, they've been there so many times that they had made a detailed map of it.

With the map memorized in Frostgem's head, he climbed up Timber's tree and started searching for an armoury. The guards that were supposed to guard the entrance to the tree were apparently assigned to be with the other soldiers protecting the perimeter.

The inside of Alpha Timber's tree wasn't that impressive. It went "straight to the point" when it comes to being the headquarters of an entire tribe, which meant that there was no grand entrance, no impressive paintings, and most of the entrances to rooms looked the same. It almost looks like just another large treehouse.

It was considered to be the most protected compound for an alpha in Torenta. There is only one small entrance and no other exit. The compound itself was shaped like a tetradecagon, or a shape with fourteen sides, and was like one large treehouse.

Even with its status as being a heavily guarded compound, ordinary TreeDwellers were still allowed in. Frostgem was an exception because most TreeDweller, if not every single one, had noticed him at least once and never thought anything of it.

Remember, AATUL, Frostgem told himself, *Avoid All The Ujanka Leaves. Actually, this might be an exception.*

The SnowLiver remained calm and kept walking until a part of him said that the door to his left was an armoury. He double-checked with his mind just to make sure that he wouldn't stumble into the room where Tree military leaders were preparing retaliation against the WaterLivers.

Once quadruple checking with himself, Frostgem carefully opened the door. It *was* an armoury, but there were two soldiers in there getting ready to defend.

"Er, can I get a weapon?" Frostgem asked, "I'm helping defend, too."

One of the soldiers sighed. "Take my backup Flux-23. Not like I need it."

Frostgem thanked the soldier and then hurried out of the room. Because he had forgotten the way out, it took him more than ten minutes to find the stairs inside a tree.

The SnowLiver then went to find where most of the soldiers were. The screamers had gotten considerably gotten quieter, with some getting calm enough to join the defense.

"I'm going to go scout," Frostgem told a random soldier.

"Stay here," the soldier said. "We have enough spies and they're reporting suspicious activity from the south side of Redwood Village, so go there."

Frostgem took the order without hesitation and headed to the other side of the village.

"Oh, so you're using a Flux-23," another soldier observed.

"Uh, yeah," Frostgem replied, "this is supposed to be a long-range bow, right?"

"Yes, so I want you to go atop that lookout post up in that tree behind us."

Knowing that he would be contributing to getting the TreeDwellers the edge during the early stages of the war, Frostgem motivated himself to go to the lookout post, which was a platform with obtuse walls and some openings to shoot arrows through. The stairs leading up to it were inside the tree that the post was built around, just like Alpha Timber's tree.

In the lookout post there was only one wolf, who was apparently one of the four commanders of the TreeDweller military.

The commander noticed Frostgem a minute after Frostgem stepping onto the platform.

"I think I know you," said the commander. "Are you like that one SnowLiver who lives near here?"

"I don't know any other SnowLivers living inside TreeDweller territory, so I guess," he replied.

"And I assume one of the generals down there told you to come here, especially because you have a Flux-23."

"Is that a general?"

"Yes. Oh, and by the way, if you don't know me, I'm Eucalyptus."

At that moment, who Frostgem assumed was a messenger informed Commander Eucalyptus of strange activity near Maple Lake and the southern area of the village.

"Tell Alpha Timber to dispatch more soldiers to the south side," Eucalyptus told the messenger. "As for Maple Lake, we can leave that area exposed until we get more information—"

The three wolves in the lookout post heard battle cries in the distance. They were too far to be TreeDweller soldiers, so everyone became worried.

"Change of orders," Eucalyptus said. "Tell our alpha to bring every single soldier remaining to the south side."

The messenger nodded and rushed out of the lookout post. The battle cries were still going on.

"As for you, SnowLiver—"

"It's Frostgem, Commander Eucalyptus."

"As for you, Frostgem, you are now on full alert. Anyone who looks like a WaterLiver, —shoot them. One more thing, I'm going to go to another lookout post. If anyone else comes in here, tell them that I told you to be the only one here, and that's if they don't have the same bow as you."

Frostgem nodded reluctantly because he would be about to kill twenty-five or so WaterLiver soldiers. He watched Eucalyptus go down the stairs and exit the tree before returning to scout.

The SnowLiver scouted in silence without any battle cries for almost half an hour when a messenger appeared out of nowhere.

"Commander Eucalyptus! Oh."

"He's at another lookout post," Frostgem informed the messenger. "Also, leave me alone because I'm on full alert."

"Thanks for letting me know," said the messenger.

The messenger left, leaving Frostgem alone once again.

The next hour was quite boring. There the regular chattering from the wolves below him as well as the rustling of leaves and the chirping of birds. Frostgem realized that holding the Flux-23 was making his arms tired, so he set the bow down in a corner. *Is this some kind of joke the TreeDweller army's pulling on me?* he wondered. *I might go back down in five minutes—*

"CHARGE!!" someone exclaimed on the ground.

Frostgem instantly forgot about going down to the ground and picked up his Flux-23. He didn't know if a Water or Tree said "charge," but it triggered him to arm himself.

Frostgem started to scan the now-battlefield for any WaterLivers. If the TreeDwellers just stayed in formation, he would have easily picked off at least three soldiers. Unfortunately for him, the Trees *broke* the formation and were now all over the place. Frostgem didn't want to accidentally kill anyone on his side.

As he was scanning the right side of the battlefield, Frostgem gave a quick glance to the left side. He didn't think anything of it and returned to scanning the right side. But all of a sudden, his Flux-23 involuntarily shifted to the left, and no matter how hard he tried to get his arm to move to the other side, Frostgem's arms were locked to the left side.

Frostgem gave up looking to the right side and instead started to scan the left side. He noticed a WaterLiver shouting orders to her comrades. *Hold on, that's Alpha Atoll,* he realized, *or maybe just another Water soldier.*

Without hesitation, he grabbed an arrow, put it onto his bow, and fired his shot.

Chapter 9

"My mother needs you in her compound right now," Scoria told Obsidian.

"I need sleep and it's not even sunrise," said Obsidian. "Aren't you also tired?"

"Yes, I am, but that's the alpha's orders."

"Fine. I'm coming in less than five minutes."

Scoria left Obsidian on his own. Just five hours before, they had arrived at the capital city of the LavaLivers, where Obsidian got a new hut gifted by Alpha Coulee. It was basically his old hut but newer.

Obsidian threw himself out of his hut and headed north toward Coulee's compound. *There are a lot more soldiers here*, he thought. *Either another conflict is happening or it's just the capital city.*

"Ah, you must be Obsidian," a guard at the entrance said. "The alpha is in the military logistics room C, and you can find it when you take a left, then a right, then three lefts and two rights."

The guard opened the door for Obsidian, who was barely making his way to the room because he kept forgetting the directions. After the second left, the path went underground, becoming significantly cooler.

Continuing to follow the directions, Obsidian saw Scoria as he made the final right. She greeted him and let him in.

Inside the logistics room, there wasn't much. On a wall was nothing but a detailed map of Torenta. In the center was a small wooden table with what looked like letters, and sitting behind it was the LavaLiver alpha.

"Glad you could make it, Obsidian," Coulee said. "I won't start the report, but rather my daughter will. Scoria."

"Right. Six days ago, our spies were sending in reports of the alpha of the WaterLivers, Atoll, declaring war on the other seven tribes. This speculation was lengthened by CanyonDweller spies who were in the same area a day later. Roughly three hours after the war ended and sixteen hours ago, Alpha Atoll *did* declare war, first on the SnowLivers and the TrenchLivers, and the other five tribes followed shortly afterward.

"This has been a big shock to all of Torenta, especially to each of the tribes' armies. We want to get prepared as soon as possible, and we have so far, initiating almost all our troops to Water territory with the rest defending the capital."

"This is where you come in, Obsidian," Coulee said. "Due to your Pymarto powers potentially benefiting our tribe and perhaps even our side of the war, I have decided to enlist you into the LavaLiver military. You will be stationed in HillDweller territory, near what is the Four-Tribe academy."

"So this report is just all about me being enlisted into the military," Obsidian said. "But just one question: why?"

"Because you have Pymarto powers and they can benefit our military," Scoria replied. "Did you even listen?"

"Well, not really. I *did* pay attention to the 'this has been a big shock to all of Torenta' part, though."

Alpha Coulee sighed. "You and Scoria will be in the Opal Division, with you being on the frontlines and Scoria working as a temporary general only for that battle."

"But why HillDweller territory?" Obsidian asked. "Can't we be initiated to TrenchLiver territory? The trenches there will protect us."

"There are no predicted battles that are going to happen in Trench territory, and under *my* orders you are to be in the Opal Division. Go now, the rest of the division is waiting."

Obsidian and Scoria left the logistics room, with Obsidian being frustrated by the fact that his alpha was taking advantage of his powers.

"The military barracks are on the west side of the compound," Scoria said.

The military barracks were large tarp domes meant to be sleeping quarters grouped into one barbed-wire area. At the entrance of each dome were signs with each division name: Lapis, Limestone, Diamond, Geode, Emerald, Gold, and Opal.

The Opal barracks was the second smallest barracks, with the Geode barracks only being slightly smaller than Opal's. Inside the quarters were what looked like very uncomfortable linen bunkbeds, a pipe with a puncture in it for ventilation, and six large water buckets. There were also bones from animals that were probably eaten a year ago. There were soldiers gearing up and an ungodly amount of spears and bows.

"Ah, is this Obsidian?" someone asked.

Obsidian looked to his left to see a shaggy wolf who had maroon ears and a charcoal-colored body.

"Yes, he is," Scoria answered. "Obsidian, this is General Quartz. He'll be one of the two generals leading you to Hill territory. The other is me."

"So, do you have any military experience, Obsidian?" Quartz asked him.

"Well, I can say that I've run away from different militaries," Obsidian replied.

"Close enough. Scoria, do you know if we have any extra Restinaps?"

"No, as far as I know. Although the Trench-Liver Ministry of Defense did send us fifty extra Osprey-37s the other day. And as usual, we have a ton of Polambo-Type 2s, as usual."

General Quartz and Scoria kept talking about military-related subjects such as food rations, the route to the soon-to-be battlefield, and the geographical features of the area. As they were talking, Obsidian tried to find a bed he could just lie down on. His day had already gone off to a wrong start; he was woken up early, Alpha Coulee enlisted him into the LavaLiver military, and he was now in a military barracks that smelled like rotten lamb.

"Attention everyone," Quartz called. "Yesterday, the LavaLivers declared war on all of Torenta. One of their first offensives will be in HillDweller territory, near the Four-Tribe Academy. We want to shut the WaterLivers down, make them start the war off on the wrong paw. We shall defeat the WaterLivers!"

Everyone cheered in response.

"General Quartz and I have already found a way to the battlefront," said Scoria. "We will head east to the coastline, and we're going to follow it south until we get to HillDweller territory. Then, after traversing the Hill landscape, we will join onto the Highland Roadway. This roadway will get us directly to what would probably be the battlefield."

"All right, get into your subgroups," General Quartz announced. "We will leave in less than ten minutes."

All of a sudden, everyone made five different groups of twenty. Within a minute, everyone was in a subgroup, making Obsidian the only wolf not belonging to a group.

"Obsidian, you can go to the subgroup with the meteor banner," Quartz told him.

The Pymarto awkwardly walked to the group, with more than a hundred pairs of eyes staring at him. Once he reached the subgroup, the soldiers were greeted by "excuse me" and "pardon," as Obsidian was trying to blend in with the fully-grown wolves.

The next ten minutes were filled with the soldiers trying to figure out which of the five subgroups would lead. Obsidian's group wanted to be the "ear" group, which he later learned meant that they were in the second group in the formation.

After those ten minutes were up, General Quartz announced that they would be on their way to the battlefield. All the subgroups lined up in the order that they picked, and soon they headed out of the barracks.

The first couple of hours of the march were not that uneventful. The division went through the familiar hot, cloudy, and dry landscape of LavaLiver territory. After three-and-a-half hours, they reached a sign that said: Now entering TreeDweller territory.

Then, it became much cooler but still relatively hot. At around the four-hour mark, the division stopped near a river to drink. Obsidian never got food rations provided by either Scoria or General Quartz, so he proceeded to get a salmon and a trout from the river.

After forty-five minutes of stopping at the river, Scoria announced that they should be moving now.

"But first, I need to make an announcement," she said. "Our original plan was to stay near, or if possible, on the TreeDweller coastline. However, General Quartz just scouted the area and has reported that there was allegedly a landslide deemed unsafe to cross. Therefore, we have taken into consideration that we should pass the Maple Lake area. Three minutes, everyone."

The soldiers regrouped again, and before they knew it, they were off marching again.

Half an hour later, the Opal division saw the waters of Maple Lake. The soldiers were looking at it, wondering just why it looked so majestic.

That awe faded when they saw what looked like meteorites falling from the sky. Everyone was panicking, but fortunately they fled from the area, calmly, without harm.

The rest of the march was pretty boring. The division did go back to their original route, trekking through HillDweller territory, passing tiny rural villages along the way.

A few hours later, the soldiers found their way to the Highland Roadway, which was a wide cobblestone road with some kind of yellow dye, splitting the roadway into two. It looked surprisingly unworn despite it being a warzone for an entire thirty-six-year war.

Wow, this is getting kind of boring, thought Obsidian, *is this what Solar had to endure when he was in the military? If so, I kind of feel bad for him.*

All was looking and feeling fine before their enemy ambushed them.

Solar looked at his family, concerned. "There's no WaterLivers on our left, we can flee."

"You sure?" Caracal asked. "There's a decent amount in all directions."

"I have two spears and a bow in my sleeping room," said Ferret, "perhaps you and I can have the spears while Solar gets the bow since he has more combat experience–"

"I found them," Solar told them. "Father, you have a Ęutanxkŷ-5 as a bow? Where did you get it?"

"Er, Gila, that one annoying merchant."

"Gila's always unreliable." Solar handed out the spears to his sibling and father.

"I'm pretty sure we can all agree that we should go out from the right," Caracal said.

"There's a big gap there as a weakness," Solar agreed.

The three carefully exited their house, moving to the back of the building. There, they lay flat and started crawling. As they were crawling through the sand, Solar drew his bow back, ready to fire an arrow. When he didn't see an arrow take out a Water-Liver, he grew confused. *Why didn't the arrow hit the WaterLiver?* Solar wondered, *it was well aimed. Maybe the wind threw it off course, just like how that arrow missed that one RPN soldier.*

Solar drew back his bow again, and when the WaterLiver soldier wasn't harmed at all, he grew even more confused. *Oh, Father never kept arrows; he only kept the bow,* he realized.

He confronted Ferret, still staying low to the ground.

"Did you even keep arrows for the bow?" Solar asked him.

"Shoot," Ferret replied, "I didn't. Oh well, Gila didn't sell arrows anyway."

The three wolves kept advancing until two WaterLiver soldiers were directly on their sides. After the soldiers were a considerable distance away from them, they took off.

About twenty minutes later, when they were in the middle of the desert, Ferret, Solar, and Caracal were trying to find an ideal place to sleep. They were actually in the middle of nowhere with the only building they saw being Alpha Sandstone's compound. In the sky, more flaming tumbleweeds were falling from the sky, meaning that more towns were being attacked.

After a few minutes of searching for an ideal resting place, Ferret found a small group of dunes that formed a protective bowl. The three wolves settled down and slept.

Part Two

A New War Breaks Out

Chapter 10

The next day, Ferret, Solar, and Caracal all woke up bright and early. They decided to go back to Lesenk to see if their house and town were okay.

Once at Lesenk, the wolves realized that almost all the town's residents were captured. At this time of day, not a lot of wolves were active, but still, there should have been a decent amount of wolves awake.

"Meerkat, is that you?" Ferret asked. Meerkat was Ferret's neighbor.

"Yes," Meerkat replied. "You didn't get captured?"

"Luckily. We went east. Also, do you think Atoll declared war on us?"

"They did, against every other tribe, too. I went west to Alpha Sandstone's compound."

Meerkat and Ferret went back and forth with each other, while Solar and Caracal went back into their house to find something to eat.

"What's in the storage room?" Solar asked Caracal.

"Nothing much," she informed Solar. "All the usual food you'd find in DustDweller territory: jackrabbits, lizards, ferrets, although Father doesn't touch them."

Solar laughed, then checked the pantry. Despite Caracal's description of it, there were a single jackrabbit and ferret. He wasn't feeling that hungry, so he opted for the ferret.

"You should really stock up on food," Solar told Caracal through chewed ferret.

"Really?" she asked.

"Yeah, there's only a jackrabbit in there because I ate the last ferret fox."

After a few minutes of eating, what Solar and Caracal thought was Ferret was actually a messenger.

"Uh, is anyone by the names of Solar and Caracal in this residence?" the messenger asked.

"We're both here," Solar replied.

"Good. Apparently, Commander Raven wants Solar back in the military," the messenger told them. "And since Caracal's general left the army, she will be assigned to the Rattlesnake Division with Solar."

"Just why?" Solar asked. "If I went AWOL, then why do they want me back?"

"Commander *Raven* wants you back," she clarified. "And on top of that, he wants you and Caracal as soon as possible."

The messenger slid out of the house, leaving the two to discuss whether they should really go back to the military.

"If we do go back to the military, then we'd both just get kicked out again!" Solar exclaimed.

"Assuming that the WaterLivers declared war on us, we can get them off on the wrong paw," Caracal countered. "Besides, I was RUSC, so I should be fine anyway."

"It's just a single division. How can less than fifty wolves defeat an entire army?"

"We're probably getting help from other tribes and divisions."

Solar sighed. "I guess you're right. We should head to Sandstone's compound."

The two exited the house and saw Ferret and Meerkat still talking. When Caracal told her father that she and Solar were leaving for the military, Ferret surprisingly said that it was okay for them to re-enlist in the military only if they came back alive when they got released.

The family said goodbye to each other with Ferret still talking to Meerkat and the pups going west to the big building that was Alpha Sandstone's compound.

All the pups of the Four-Tribe Academy were woken up by five rings of the announcement bell, which meant that there was going to be an announcement in the grand lobby. Tempest and Thundergiver were among the last pups to arrive there, as they already knew that the announcement Alpine was about to give was related to the new war.

"Everyone, quiet down," Alpine told the pups. "Yesterday, word broke out saying that Atoll, the alpha of the WaterLivers, has declared war on all seven tribes of Torenta, which includes the tribes that surround our academy. By the way, if you have never heard, the day before, the old war ended. I know that I have granted most of your requests to leave the academy during the old war, but I think that during this war, I shouldn't grant any of those requests if that means that my students could be harmed."

Most of the pups whined in response.

"Now, most of you might be thinking that you might not see your pack during back-home leave. There will be just an annual back-home leave that's double the amount of days as one semi-annual back-home leave. And as for you WaterLivers, I will try to figure something out for you guys. That's the end of my announcement. No classes for today and tomorrow, so you are free to go around the academy as you wish."

The mood in the grand lobby lightened a little bit after Alpine said the second part of his announcement. After that, everyone went either outside or back to their dens.

Thundergiver and Tempest both agreed to go outside, just to get some fresh air. Apparently, most of the pups decided to go outside, too.

When the two pups went outside, they were instantly greeted by a gust of wind.

They were next greeted by half of the Water-Liver army to the left.

In most militaries, this only meant that about a few hundred soldiers would be present.

Since three-quarters of all WaterLivers are in the army, that meant that thousands of soldiers would be present because the tribe is the most populous.

All the pups outside were frightened by the fact that five thousand WaterLiver soldiers were less than a kilometer away, so they started screaming and headed inside the building. The pups inside got confused, then started to scream as well.

A couple of minutes later, Alpine decided to address everything that was going on.

"Everyone, please calm down," he called, although no one listened. "They are not going to harm us. For safety, everyone go back to your dens–"

Eight massive boulders crashed into the academy from the sky.

Frostgem's arrow hit the WatcrLiver soldier dead on in the eye. It really only took less than three seconds for the arrow to hit the soldier, but to him it felt like more than three hours. A fellow soldier came up to them. They were yelling a name that was definitely not "Atoll," so Frostgem became disappointed. *Hey, Frostgem, a kill is a kill*, he told himself.

Over the next half an hour, the TreeDwellers and Frostgem kept the heat up against the WaterLivers. While the Waters were taking casualties, the TreeDwellers' biggest injury was two soldiers getting moderately cut.

Finally, at around High Sun, the general of the WaterLivers' side decided to retreat north. As the Trees were celebrating, Frostgem decided that it was time to come down and celebrate with them.

During the celebrations, Alpha Timber, who was overseeing the battle from his tree, congratulated everyone for contributing to their winning the battle.

"But it's not over yet," he said. "You can all celebrate now, but trust me, the WaterLivers will come back."

Timber kept yammering about whether some non-military residents wanted to enlist in the military. Frostgem obviously didn't want to, so he just excused himself to go back to his hut.

The rest of the day for Frostgem was just fishing at Maple Lake and stocking up on other foods. Then, during the evening, he wondered if he could see what Thundergiver and Tempest were up to.

But they're in the Four-Tribe Academy, Frostgem realized. *If only I could enroll myself into it...*

Then, a very bright idea came to his brain.

Maybe I can just straight up ask the head of the academy if I can join! What was his name... Alpine? Right. Alpine knows me from that time we went into my bunker while getting away from Atoll.

After a few moments of pondering, Frostgem realized that it wouldn't be that impossible to do. Whenever Alpine exits the main building, he could come up to him, reintroduce himself to Alpine, his situation, and then ask if he could join.

Double-checking if he should really enroll at the Four-Tribe Academy, Frostgem stuffed his stomach with fish and otter and set out to the academy.

Obviously, no one was expecting an ambush this far east, so wolves started panicking at first. Luckily, before things got out of hand, the LavaLivers fought back. Because the ambushers only had a quarter as many wolves as the division did, they quickly retreated within ten minutes.

From that encounter, nothing out of the ordinary happened. Arguably the strangest thing that happened was when two rabbits attacked a soldier. The soldier killed them both and happily ate them as snacks.

At around sunset, the division reached what General Quartz said was the "support lines." There wasn't really anything marking the "support lines," as it was just a group of shrubs and tall grasses.

"All the shovelers, start shoveling the trenches," Quartz told a group of soldiers.

During the march, Obsidian always wondered why a group of fifteen wolves had shovels and the others didn't. Now, his question was answered.

In the distance, Obsidian saw the Four-Tribe academy, sitting on top of sort of like a mini plateau. For whatever reason, there were holes in the roof of the main building.

On Obsidian's left-to-back side, a small tarp tent was being made. He wondered why there was a lone tent in the middle of nothing, but as he was about to ask, a wolf put up a sign in front of it saying, Generals And Commanders Only. Do Not Enter Without Permission.

"Dinnertime," General Quartz announced un-enthusiastically. "Remember that food rations are tight, so don't ask for extras from other wolves."

The rest of the division nodded, while Obsidian went up to Quartz to ask him for food rations.

"Don't ask me," he said. "You should've gotten food rations with the other—"

"He actually didn't get any," Scoria interrupted. "Since he had a last-minute enlistment, the wolves at the MFDC, the Military Food Distribution Center, didn't get his rations in time."

"Very well," General Quartz sighed. "Go hunt a rabbit or something."

Without hesitation, Obsidian took off, desperately trying to find a rabbit, or anything to eat. After twenty minutes, he gave up and instead ate some berries he found in a nearby bush.

While searching for food, Obsidian did some scouting, too. He learned that the enemy was already there and in fact was settled in.

"General Quartz!" he exclaimed. "I have, er, a scouting report for you."

Quartz emerged from the "generals only" tent. "I didn't *ask* you to scout. Although I still want to listen to it, though."

"The WaterLivers are already here," Obsidian informed him, "they seem to be already settled in. I assume they haven't spotted us."

"Did you check how many soldiers they had?" he asked.

"That's hard," said Obsidian, "though if I had to guess...a few thousand?"

Both Scoria's and Quartz's eyes widened. "Scoria, we might need to send one of our messengers back to Alpha Coulee. Tell the messenger that we might need reinforcements from the Emerald Division, maybe even the TrenchLivers if necessary."

"I already assessed Obsidian's report and therefore sent a messenger to Alpha Coulee saying that we need reinforcements from the Emerald Division."

"Hold on, did you guys catch that noise?" Obsidian asked them.

"Yeah, I *think* I heard the word 'charge,'" Scoria answered. "Wait."

Then, shortly afterward, came the charging footsteps of half the WaterLiver military.

Chapter 11

Caracal and Solar arrived at Alpha Sand-stone's compound with virtually nobody inside it. The only wolves they actually saw were diplomats, ready to leave the compound.

"Why isn't anybody here?" Solar asked. "I definitely remember the compound having way more wolves inside it."

"I don't have a viable guess, but I believe that most wolves in here are military-related," Caracal said.

"But what does that have to do with nobody being here?"

"The new war broke out a couple of days before," she replied, "and because of that, perhaps Alpha Sandstone initiated the entire military."

"Whatever," Solar sighed, "we should head to the barracks right now."

The two pups took twenty minutes to find the barracks due to the compound's immense size. They expected to find them filled with soldiers, but when they went into the barracks, Solar and Caracal only found one wolf in there.

"Hey, Cacti," Caracal said, "we came here because Commander Raven re-enlisted me and Solar in the military. Do you know where they are?"

"If it was the Rattlesnake division...approximately southeastern Trench territory, but that's just a rough estimate," Cacti replied. Cacti was the military barracks logistics manager, staying in the barracks for most of his day to keep it clean and to sometimes repair stuff.

"So they left without us," said Solar.

"Yes. Unfortunately."

"So what are we left to do now?" he asked Cacti.

"I assume you've never read the DustDweller Military Rulebook, or the DDMR," said Cacti.

Both Solar and Caracal shook their heads.

"Lucky you guys, because I read the whole 629-page rulebook. Thrice," Cacti told them. "Section Q.304.12D, which is on page 420, states that 'any soldiers re-enlisted by a commander, alpha, general, lieutenant, pack member, etc., who have been RUSC, IESOT, EWAP, JTOT, LPOITT, TWOPI, RWEE, PLOSCO, OSHOT, VENUL, KIAUDD, RF-BIC, LONGOT, or AWOL when they were active, and are late to a battle, offensive, operation, etc. could be required to do one of two things: (1) de-enlisted from the military again, or (2) go to the battle by themselves.' And you know Commander Raven; he doesn't like number ones. So I guess you two are supposed to go to the battlefront by yourselves."

"We don't have a choice," Caracal told Solar. "Let's go."

"Cacti, one more question," said Solar, "where *will* the battlefield be?"

"I think they said something about being near the Four-Tribe Academy or something," Cacti replied.

"Solar, we *actually* need to be going now," Caracal said.

Caracal and Solar said goodbye to Cacti and headed south. Their plan was to go through the center of TreeDweller territory to stop at Maple Lake a little after High Sun, then keep walking through Tree territory until they got to the Four-Tribe Academy.

At around an hour after sunset, the two pups arrived at the battlefield. They knew they were in the right place when they saw many WaterLivers and LavaLivers fighting in the wide meadow below them.

"We're definitely at the place," Caracal said.

"Yeah, I also see the Four-Tribe Academy on my right, on that plateau," Solar agreed. "But where's our division?"

Caracal tried looking for any DustDwellers on the battlefield, but saw no DustDweller colors. After some looking, she saw a small group of yellow and gold near the eastern horizon.

"I think I found our division," she informed Solar.

"Really? Nothing strange to me," he said. "Okay, *now* I see it."

Caracal's theory was confirmed by a group of about eighty DustDwellers all around what looked like a blue banner with a snake on it.

"I'm going to teleport there," Solar said suddenly.

"You can't," Caracal told him.

"Say, 'teal snake.'"

"Teal...snake?"

"Raven."

All of a sudden, they were smack in the middle of the Rattlesnake Division.

"Huh? How did you do that—"

"Solar?" Someone asked.

"Hey! Woodrat! Great to see you again," Solar said.

"How did you get here—"

"Just stay silent and don't ask."

Ten minutes later, the division came to a stop at the eastern side of the battlefield, right next to the LavaLivers. The only thing splitting the two tribes was an array of decently sized hills.

"All right, Rattlesnakes, set up everything within three minutes," Commander Raven announced. "We're going to charge right after."

In a sudden flurry, there were tents being made, weapons flying all around, and Commander Raven shouting out random things for no reason.

"We're done settling, I believe," Raven said. "So, I need everyone to fight for not themselves, but their tribe. Also, I do not care if any of you guys make it back here when I tell you to retreat. Charge!!"

After that, the battle now had a mix of gold and yellow. It seemed like everybody funneled out of the camp they made less than five minutes ago.

Everybody except Caracal and Solar.

"Ah, if it isn't Ferret's pups, Solar and Caracal," Commander Raven said. "Now, I won't get mad at you for not going into the battle if you tell me how you got here."

"We came into the barracks, where we saw Cacti there," Caracal replied.

"Hm. Cacti. And?"

"We asked him where the Rattlesnake Division went, and he said that they were heading to an area near the Four-Tribe Academy," Solar added.

"Just straight up asking questions," the commander remarked, "All right. I won't throw you into the battle at the moment. Go scout. Caracal goes to the left side and Solar goes to the right. I want you both back in an hour and a half. If not, I'll assume you're dead."

The two nodded and headed to their respective sides.

As Solar was attempting to scout, he realized that there *was* nothing to scout. *Nothing to scout,* he thought, *though I do believe that Tempest and*

Thundergiver attend the Four-Tribe Academy. I could spend an hour or so there.

Solar went up the plateau where the academy was, thinking that he just made a genius idea.

That's when he saw the locked main entrance.

At around an hour after High Sun, Frostgem could see the Four-Tribe Academy. During the walk there, he always doubted himself on whether or not he actually wanted to join the Four-Tribe Academy. His walk was full of "actually not" and "maybe I actually want to do this."

In the distance, he could see a ton of Water-Liver soldiers, which made Frostgem slightly concerned.

Right, all I need to do is just walk up to Alpine and ask him if I can just join the academy, Frostgem told himself.

That's when he saw the locked doors. *Weird,* he thought, *I guess I'll have to get in another way.*

He started to survey the area around the academy, but he didn't have to look far because there were large holes on the roof of the main building.

At first Frostgem thought that it would be practically impossible to get on the roof, and it would be just as hard to descend into the academy safely.

That's when he noticed a random wood plank, going from the roof all the way to the ground. It was as if the plank was saying, "Frostgem, I'm definitely making your life easier now."

Frostgem took advantage of the plank and easily climbed up to the roof.

That was the first step done; now all he had to do was just descend without problem. Unfortunately, there was no other way than to just straight up go down thirty feet, so Frostgem winged it.

The fall wasn't as bad as he thought.

That was before this thing called "the impact" reached him.

Frostgem's bones almost snapped, but they managed not to fracture or dislocate.

Then he started sliding.

He couldn't process why at first, but after sliding hind legs first, Frostgem realized that he landed on a boulder, which he later assumed caused the hole in the roof.

After quickly reading the minds of sixteen pups, Frostgem assessed what was going on. Most of the pups were thinking about the WaterLiver soldiers he saw earlier attacking them, and others were assuring themselves that they wouldn't get attacked.

The next thing Frostgem had to do was to find Alpine.

That was pretty hard because the Four-Tribe Academy was huge in size.

Alpine might be in his den, Frostgem thought, *or, as they called it, an "office."*

It took Frostgem twenty minutes to find Alpine's den. Even though he entered the den, he didn't see Alpine anywhere.

That's a little strange, he wondered, *if he isn't here, then I could just visit Thundergiver and Tempest.*

Then it took Frostgem another ten minutes to find the dens of the pups. They were in two different dens, and each den was shared by three pups.

This was what the writing to the left of Thundergiver's den said:

G-5

Sunfish

Birchleaf

Thundergiver

This was what the writing to the left of Tempest's den said:

G-6

Milkweed

Tempest

Foliage

Frostgem decided to go into Thundergiver's den first, and the first thing he saw was a frightened TreeDweller, followed by a frightened WaterLiver and a slightly less frightened Thundergiver.

"Frostgem, you know you're going to get kicked out of the academy if you stay here for too long," Thundergiver told Frostgem.

"Yes, I know, but I'm trying to enroll myself into the Four-Tribe Academy," he replied.

"SnowLiver, or Frostgem, whatever Thundergiver just called you, you can't just enroll yourself into the academy," the WaterLiver added, "you also have to be either a WaterLiver like me, a TrenchLiver like Thundergiver, a TreeDweller like Birchleaf, or a HillDweller to join, and you clearly are a SnowLiver."

"Well, I don't care anyway," said Frostgem, "I just need to know where Alpine is. I couldn't find him in his den."

"Then try the library," the TreeDweller offered.

"Okay." Frostgem exited the den in search of the library.

He didn't have to walk much. In fact, he didn't even have to walk to the library because Alpine was right in front of him.

"Ah! Indigo! What are you doing here?" Alpine asked. "Go back to your...oh. Wait...am I dreaming?"

"No, you aren't," Frostgem told him.

"You're that one SnowLiver that helped me escape Alpha Atoll that one time...was it Frostgem?"

"Yes," he replied.

"Okay, but how and why are you here?"

"I want to enroll myself into your academy," Frostgem said suddenly.

"I'm sorry, Frostgem, but you can't. You have to be from one of the four tribes that surround the academy. Hence, the Four-Tribe Academy."

"I've already got that from Sunfish. Listen. I'm an orphan, or at least I think I am, who was left in TreeDweller territory. During the old war, most TreeDwellers avoided me, and later I *did* want to get avoided. That's when Thundergiver and Tempest came out of nowhere and helped me come out of my solitary life in the middle of the TreeDweller wilderness. When the war ended, they came back here to continue life here. Earlier today, I got inspired by them to come here to enroll. Also, I *have lived* in Tree territory for pretty much my entire life, so that technically counts, right?"

Alpine sighed. "You can be enrolled into my academy just because you lived in one territory for almost your entire life? Although I suppose that that's a good loophole you found. You're enrolled into the Four-Tribe Academy."

Chapter 12

"We shouldn't wait for the WaterLivers," said Scoria, "we need our soldiers to go in now."

General Quartz nodded. He went out of the tent and yelled, "Charge!!"

Then, a flurry of maroon, red, dark orange, and black LavaLivers joined the blue, green, and white WaterLivers.

Meanwhile, Obsidian was still in the general's tent.

"Aren't you going to join the battle, Obsidian?" Scoria asked him.

"Er...my claws don't do that much damage to WaterLivers; I need a weapon," he replied.

"Oh, right," said Scoria, "we forgot to bring those extra Ospreys with us. Just wait here in our tent and General Quartz will figure something out for you."

General Quartz didn't come back until three hours later. Within those three hours, a DustDweller military division came and another TrenchLiver division was approaching, too.

After those three hours, Scoria explained that Obsidian didn't have a weapon.

"He doesn't need one," Quartz said sternly. "The reason why he got enlisted was because he already has one!"

"Which is?" Scoria asked.

"Come on, you didn't get it? The whole reason Alpha Coulee enlisted him was because of his Pymarto powers!"

"Er, I didn't remember," Scoria lied, "anyway, General Quartz, can he operate from the trenches and not on the battlefield?"

"You're a pathetic general," he mumbled. "Fine, he can. He can stay with the crossbows. They're to your right, Obsidian."

"Uh, okay." Obsidian went to the right where he saw a group of about ten soldiers, with crossbows over the edge of the trenches.

"Hey, you don't have a crossbow," said one of the soldiers.

"Well, then check this out. For context, I'm a Pymarto." Obsidian lifted his head up, and then a group of six WaterLivers started floating in the air in the distance. He then rested his head and the WaterLivers were flung back to their camp in the west.

"That's definitely not you," another LavaLiver scoffed.

"Oh yeah?" Obsidian mimicked, "what kind of ordinary wolf can make six soldiers levitate, then get flung a kilometer away?"

"Okay, okay, geez. If you can do that, can you fling all of the WaterLivers away?"

"It's hard, but I can try," said Obsidian.

"I mean, there's no way he can–"

"Green polar bear. Green polar bear."

A few thousand WaterLivers rose into the sky, confused about why they were forty feet off the ground.

"Yellow moth."

The WaterLiver soldiers were flung northward, and perhaps some unlucky Waters landed in TrenchLiver territory.

"Okay, now *that* was you," one of the soldiers gaped.

I mean, that's understandable, Solar thought; *academies* do *need privacy. But think! What would Frostgem do in this situation?*

That's when Solar noticed the wood plank and the hole and decided to walk up the plank and drop into the hole on the roof, which was exactly what Frostgem had done a few hours before.

After dropping into the academy, Solar decided to stroll around the empty academy. *Why is the academy empty?* Solar wondered: *if the Four-Tribe*

Academy is a bustling academy, then why is it empty?

After some more walking, Solar connected the dots: the stone that fell from the sky frightened the pups into taking shelter in some place.

During the walk, Solar continued to find interesting things that at least he'd never seen before. This included the history den, the library, a prey center, classrooms, and even an area made just for eating.

Solar quickly got bored after that. He only had twenty minutes before his curfew, so he had to find Thundergiver and Tempest quickly.

That was before he saw a hallway full of what looked like dens, and Solar's suspicion was confirmed by a stone carving that said Student Den Complexes. Dens A1-L8.

I just hope Tempest and Thundergiver's dens are both in this hallway, Solar thought. *Well, if there's letters, then it'll probably go to Z8.*

He then started to search the dens in hopes of either of those two being in any of the dens. He realized that each den held three pups inside them, so he was going to concentrate a lot harder to notice the names.

Finally, at the G-5 den, he saw Thundergiver's name on it. He immediately was greeted by a Tree-Dweller, a WaterLiver that looked nothing like Tempest, and Thundergiver.

"I must be dreaming again," Not Tempest mumbled.

"You aren't," Thundergiver told Not Tempest, "and Solar! Are you trying to enroll yourself like Frostgem not long ago?"

"You can enroll yourself *in* the Four-Tribe Academy?" Solar asked. "Well, no thanks. I'm in the DustDweller army."

"Oh," the TreeDweller said, "well, you should go back to your division, or whatever they call it in the military, so you don't get into trouble."

"I'm scouting for my commander, and he doesn't know that I'm here," said Solar. "Anyway, Frostgem enrolled *himself* in the academy?! I thought you needed to be from one of the four tribes that surround the academy, hence the Four-Tribe Academy."

"That was exactly what I told him, but he said that he didn't care," Not Tempest told Solar.

"Well, I need to actually scout now so that I won't get myself de-enlisted. I promise I'll come back later, Thundergiver."

"Well, Tempest doesn't know about all this, so make sure you visit her, too. Or maybe I'll just tell her."

Solar said goodbye to the three pups and left.

Now all he had to do was find a way out of the academy.

This was especially difficult because the place he came in from was only a one-way entrance.

Then Solar realized something: one of the academy's sides didn't exist. He was pretty sure that this was meant to be because it would directly lead outside to the area that the pups usually play in.

Solar ran to the opening, where he exited the main building to actually start scouting. He knew that he had less than five minutes to actually scout, so he looked for something that would probably catch Commander Raven's attention.

WaterLivers who looked like they were of high honor caught Solar's eyes first. He obviously knew that telling Raven that there were four generals at the WaterLiver camp would irritate him, so Solar kept looking.

His eyes veered slightly to the right, locking onto what looked like an ordinary soldier, but his mind kept telling him, "Alpha Atoll, Alpha Atoll, Alpha Atoll."

That's when Solar knew that that would get Commander Raven's attention. So he ran back to the DustDweller camp to give him the news.

"So you've made it back alive after all," Raven said sarcastically, "and Caracal! So did you. Now, I want your reports."

"Alpha Atoll is present in the WaterLiver camp," they both said.

Raven stopped chewing his roasted cacti. "Yeah, yeah," the commander scoffed, "there is no way Alpha Atoll is here, exposed here in the front lines."

"Atoll *always* comes to battles, at least if she knows her army's going to win against the opponent," Solar countered. "Also, how are we supposed to communicate to each other that we should make up excuses from the opposite sides of the battlefield?"

"Er, tha-that's a good reason," Raven pondered, "well, you guys must have made that up while I was thinking about where to put you guys."

"If we whispered to each other, then you would have definitely heard it," said Caracal, "and we took off as soon as you told us to scout."

Commander Raven sighed. "Whatever, you can relax for a little bit, maybe for like an hour or so."

Caracal and Solar nodded and decided to take a power nap behind a small yet steep hill.

When the two pups started to rest, they noticed that it was a little *too* quiet.

"Is it me, or is it way quieter than it used to be?" Caracal wondered.

Solar was wondering as well, so he went up the hill they were resting on and saw no WaterLivers on the battlefield.

"Must've retreated," he concluded.

"No, Alpha Atoll wouldn't lose like that," said Caracal.

Solar looked again, this time noticing the Lava and Dusts going back casually. The first couple of soldiers even already made it back, already starting to settle in again.

"Did you guys see that?" a soldier asked.

"Yeah, one moment we were fighting to the death with them, and the other, they were levitating, and in another, they were flung so far away that I wouldn't be surprised if some even landed in TrenchLiver territory!" said another.

"Okay, we can all admit that none of us Dust-Dwellers did that, right?" someone asked.

"Yeah. If I'm being honest, one of the Lava-Livers did that."

Commander Raven emerged into the six-wolf conversation but wanted to speak to everybody. "Everyone, please listen," he announced, "we have kind of defeated the WaterLivers, though I'm not sure how. Now, knowing the WaterLivers with our past experience fighting *with* them, they will definitely come back. That's fine, anyway, because we have to stay on the battlefront for a minimum of thirty-six hours once a battle is officially declared over. Everybody will be on full alert up until then, possibly even longer. Division dismissed."

All the soldiers kept talking, with some going into their tents. Solar and Caracal went to ask Commander Raven for a tent because they joined the division via teleporting.

"Lucky we brought an extra tent with us," Raven replied, plopping a few metal bars and a long piece of burlap. "Oh, and your rations, forgot about that..."

"Exactly, Commander Raven," said Caracal, "the wolves at the food center didn't grab ours, right–"

"Eh. Your loss. Go hunt."

The two pups sighed and went to hunt.

At that moment, Frostgem knew that his life would become even better. There would be food that was already pre-hunted, there would be classes to keep himself entertained, and on top of that, he would get to spend a lot more time with Thundergiver and Tempest.

But that wouldn't be the case for a little while, as Alpine told him to stay in the library.

"Also, watch out for flying boulders crashing in from the sky," Alpine said.

Using the directions the Head Wolf told Frostgem to follow, he arrived at the library in less than three minutes.

The first thing that he did was embrace the smells of the library. All there was to smell was the general earthy smell Frostgem regularly takes in, this time without all the annoying pollen getting into his snout.

The next thing Frostgem did was look at all the tablets that made the library the library. The tablets covered everything from war reports donated by some of the alphas to how to properly eat a cow and a papaya at the same time. Occasionally, Frostgem might stumble across a papyrus scroll, probably written by CanyonDweller or WaterLiver scholars, as they had the best scholars of the last century or so.

Frostgem stayed in the library until two hours later, when Alpine called his name. Not wanting to make a bad impression on his "unofficial" first day, he came to Alpine in no time flat.

"So, after a stressful two hours and ten minutes, two upset pups, and a den to clean, I have found a den for you. If you ever noticed, there was another pup in the library, but I assume that they never saw you. Yeah, he just joined the academy a few hours before you, and he's been looking for a new den ever since. I have 'forcefully removed' the two pups who were clearing the way for you guys. And now that the den has been cleaned, you can move in! Your den is den G2, three dens down from

Thundergiver's and four from Tempest. Now, as a challenge and to get yourself adjusted to the academy, I am going to make you go on your own while I fill the other pup in on what's happening. Later."

Frostgem exited the library, with Alpine not knowing that he'd already seen the den complex.

Four minutes later, Frostgem found the den complex, with his being near the middle.

The writing on the left of the den showed the code for the den, and the names were as follows: Bluefin, Pinecone, and Frostgem. Past the fake Ujanka leaves, inside the den was already one WaterLiver whom Frostgem assumed was Bluefin. There were three types of beds, perhaps for each of the three pups occupying it: a fern bed, a moss bed, and a triple-layered burlap bed.

"Er, which bed did you take?" Frostgem asked Bluefin.

"I took the fern bed," Bluefin replied. "Wait, aren't you the SnowLiver Alpine told me I was sharing my den with?"

"Yeah," said Frostgem. "Did I offend you?"

"No, no, not at all, it's just...the fact that I've never seen a SnowLiver before."

"Oh, you've never seen *anyone* like me, ever?" Frostgem wondered.

"I lived on one of the islands that were part of the Anemone Archipelago up until I came here," said Bluefin, "and since my pack rarely leaves that island, it's rare to get to see wolves from different tribes. Even so, my first day here at the Four-Tribe Academy was the first day I officially left WaterLiver territory, since the main academy is registered under the HillDwellers."

"How old are you?"

"Four."

"So in most of your four years of your existence in Torenta, you've never left Water territory?"

"Most."

Frostgem nodded, and the two sat in silence. That was before he brought up the boulder situation five minutes later.

"So, on my way here, I noticed that there were some large boulders scattered around the academy. Any info on that?" he asked.

"No, to be honest," Bluefin replied. "We students were minding our business when a few boulders came crashing down from the sky not long after that large WaterLiver army battalion appeared that's outside right now. I guess that Alpine was feeling a little bit dramatic, so he made all of us go to our rooms ASAP. Nothing much happened after that—"

Bluefin was interrupted by yet another three boulders.

Chapter 13

"Well, I'm pretty sure *something* happened past that point," Frostgem remarked.

"Why does this keep happening?" Bluefin wondered.

"Has Alpine told you guys that the WaterLivers have declared war on all the other tribes? Alpha Atoll has had a specific hatred against Alpine, so it would make sense that she would attack the academy."

"Oh yeah, good point. He did tell us, and that was earlier this morning."

The two sat in silence again when the third pup, presumably Pinecone, found the den and went inside.

"Are you guys Frostgem and Bluefin?" the TreeDweller asked.

"He's Frostgem, I'm Bluefin," Bluefin informed Pinecone. "By the way, we took both the moss and the fern beds, so you have no choice but to use the burlap bed. It's really uncomfortable, just for an FYI."

"Thanks for the intel," Pinecone nodded. "But I mean, how bad could it actually be?"

She tried lying down on the burlap bed, but immediately sprang up again.

"It's so uncomfortable!" Pinecone exclaimed.

"Sorry, first come first served," said Bluefin.

The three pups sat in silence, with Frostgem even taking a nap at one point.

Three hours later, Alpine showed up in the den complex. "So, pups, you may have seen the big boulders coming down from the sky," he announced, "and again, everything is okay as of now. When the first wave of boulders dropped, I wasn't going to let any of you pups out of your dens until probably tomorrow. Now, I have looked outside to see that the wolves that attacked us, most likely the WaterLivers, are now distracted by their enemies, the LavaLivers and the DustDwellers, both of which I requested to come here in case the Waters attacked our academy. Because of this, I will let you guys out of your dens, but only for two hours for dinner. You are free to roam around the main academy as normal, but you are prohibited from going past the fenced area even though I allowed you guys to go past it before. Anyway, Dens A1-L8 dismissed."

All of a sudden, a couple hundred pups stormed out of their dens, heading toward the direction of the grand lobby.

"This is probably the most dangerous five minutes of your life," Bluefin told the other two pups. "It's especially dangerous when Alpine makes a big announcement like the one he just made. This is because the pups have a tendency to go all out when they get to do something when they haven't done anything over the past few hours. Just brace yourselves."

Pinecone and Frostgem nodded, and the three went out into the "storm" carefully.

At first, Frostgem thought that Bluefin was being dramatic when he said "brace yourselves," but now he totally understood why. Like a riptide, Frostgem was thrown immediately forward, and in fact, he barely had to move at all. The "current" was doing all the walking for him.

Frostgem felt a little weird being so high up from all the pups. He answered his question when he later found out that the average age for a pup in the Four-Tribe Academy was a year and ten months old. Frostgem also later learned that he was one of the less than twenty pups to be over the age of four and a half.

It was smooth sailing for most of the ride, but that was before Frostgem heard Bluefin, who was about six feet away, yell. "The current's going to split up!"

The SnowLiver didn't process it fast enough to realize that Bluefin meant that the pups were going to go to different places, making him walk on his own.

The pups around Frostgem split into three different directions, and since he didn't realize that he now had to walk on his own, Frostgem fell flat on the floor. While most pups saw that he fell and evaded him, some just straight up trampled him.

Eventually, Frostgem did get up, and decided to turn left because that's where most of the pups went. He did notice that the "current" had gotten much weaker, but still to the point that he could still cruise as normal. He wasn't going to take his chances, so he walked himself.

As the pups were about to go outside, Frostgem "braced himself" again. It wasn't that bad, as the pups slowly went out of the queue instead of abruptly as when they were exiting the den complex.

As soon as Frostgem found his footing in, he immediately went to find Thundergiver and Tempest. After some searching, he did find Thundergiver. However, Tempest was nowhere to be seen.

"Thundergiver! Do you know where Tempest is?" Frostgem asked.

"I'm as clueless as you," he replied, "but knowing her, she must be in the library or history den. Also, did you get yourself a den?"

"Yes, I did. It's a few dens down from yours, apparently. I'm in G2. Also, any updates on the boulders?"

"Yeah, I've been asking myself the same question," said Thundergiver. "The best theory according to my denmates is that the WaterLiver army battalion below us attacked the academy with them."

"Heard that one too many times," Frostgem remarked. "Now that I know that you're here, can you give me a quick tour of the academy?"

"Of course. After my few years here, I can definitely transform myself into a tour guide."

The two pups started off the tour by walking around the fenced part of the outside of the academy.

"Our first area of focus is here, outside of the main academy building, also known as the recreational area. We pups have been past the fenced area many times, and earlier today was one of the few times Alpine initiated the 'stay inside of the fenced area' rule. Anyway, the recreational area is a hotspot for playing pups, and the part of the creek that's within the fenced area is a hotspot for fish, and when you go past the fence, you might be lucky enough to find and hunt a deer. You'd be respected if you caught at least three deer within your first month. Here, just to make our tour...interactive, why not catch a fish in the river?"

"This fish isn't as tasty as the ones in Maple Lake," Frostgem said.

Thundergiver and Frostgem went into the main academy, where Thundergiver introduced the second and third stops.

"Our second stop is going to be the history den. There isn't really much to do here, in my opinion. During history class, which would most likely take place here, all you do is look at the same old maps over and over again as well as memorize the names of random CanyonDweller generals whom you do not need to know about. Also, I don't think I saw Tempest, so she's probably in the library.

"On our right is Alpine's den. I assume you came here first when you were enrolling. I think that Alpine is probably busy doing things related to the boulder attacks, so it's better not to bother him right now."

"Oh, I've never seen this," Frostgem observed. "The first room or den that I technically went to was yours. Then I saw Alpine walking near some other place and talked to him that way."

The two pups went down the main hallway and took a right. This area of the academy was probably the only area where there were no boulders in sight.

"Here are some of the classrooms," Thundergiver informed Frostgem. "You probably won't be spending *any* of your time here for the next couple of days, but when Alpine says that it is safe for us pups to go back to classes, you'll be spending *all* of your time here. There are multiple different classes, which include literature, mythology, combat, and occasionally, history."

Frostgem and Thundergiver made two lefts and arrived at a den complex similar to their own.

"This is the den complex for dens M1-X8. Not like you'll come here often, just like I haven't gone here since my tenth day at the academy. But since it's part of the academy, it's part of the tour."

The two pups walked through most of the snaky hallways, with Thundergiver talking about the history of the academy, why it was founded, and its modifications over the years (the academy was fewer than twenty-five years old, so there wasn't much to talk about).

"Now, on our left is our final stop, the library. If you aren't an energetic, extroverted pup like 95 percent of everyone here, this is the place to go. It is a huge dictionary filled with pretty much every single topic spoken by a wolf, with topics ranging from iguana biology to how the CanyonDwellers lost eighty percent of their land to how to tame and not kill a bull, but that last one's outdated, as bulls on Torenta went extinct seven decades ago.

"That brings us to the end of the tour, and if you have any questions about the academy, feel free to ask me, Alpine, or Tempest, *if* we can find her. Actually, let's try to find her now."

Frostgem and Thundergiver went into the library in search of the WaterLiver. As Thundergiver had said, the library is a huge dictionary, so they had to weave through the shelves, which gained some more traffic than usual.

After about eight minutes of searching, the two pups found Tempest, towards the left of the library in the "birds of prey" section, probably trying to find some info on the continent of Kloma.

"Tempest, I knew you were going to be here," said Thundergiver.

"I couldn't find you after the announcement, so I didn't care and came here instead. And Frostgem? Are you a ghost or something?"

"Nope, real," he replied.

"How did you come here?" Tempest asked.

"I walked," Frostgem replied. "How else would I have come here?"

"There are actually many ways you could travel from point A to point B on land," she said, "you can run; you can take a horse (but you need to tame one first); you can be escorted by a military battalion, you could use a chariot..."

Tempest kept talking for another ten minutes. Meanwhile, Thundergiver and Frostgem decided to get some fish from the creek as that was the only reliable food option within the fenced area. The two pups caught a total of eleven fish in total, with Thundergiver getting three and Frostgem getting eight, probably because Thundergiver could always go to the eating hall for some pre-caught fish whereas Frostgem needed to hunt and eat fish for his own survival.

"...and finally, well, just walk," Tempest concluded. "Oh. Great. Thundergiver's left me alone again."

"Actually, I'm right here," he said. "Sheesh, these fish are slippery. My claws need to get grippier."

"We caught fish while you were rambling about ways that I could have come here," Frostgem added. "Here, take two. Thundergiver says that we should meet at the eating hall, and I *just* forgot where that is."

"It's fine.You'll get used to your surroundings within a few days," Thundergiver reassured him. "It always happens to new pups."

The three pups eventually made their way to the eating hall. The eating hall was a big maze full of tables and benches. It was just a relatively bright lit part of the academy that was cut out of one large stone. The only thing that actually stood out in the hall other than the benches and tables was some bowls full of fish and a variety of different meats.

"Okay, now that we've got the '*how* did you come here' part taken care of, *why* did you come here?" Tempest asked Frostgem.

"Well, being an orphan, at least I think I am, can be pretty boring. For example, here's my daily routine: wake up, eat some food, eat some more fifteen minutes after that, if there isn't any in storage space, I go hunt near Maple Lake, then I eat again after that, I do nothing, I eat, I do nothing, I eat again, then eat half an hour later, but that last one depends on my mood, do nothing, I eat once more, do nothing, and then sleep. Sounds boring, right?"

"Well, one thing I can say for sure is that there is a *ton* of eating involved," Tempest remarked. "You eat six times a day. SIX. And that's only if you aren't feeling good. Your parents must have a godly amount of metabolism genes just for you to just maintain a normal body weight. Although the Docosahexaenoic Acid and the protein in general coming from the common TreeDweller salmon or the Okalerkó-Yujafķa Myökė, the Two-Tribe Trout should be good enough for you–"

"Attention, pups," Alpine called to the pups in the eating hall and library, "I want everyone in their

dens as soon as possible. There is a huge swarm of...
birds, and they might attack us. Do not panic."

Everyone panicked.

Chapter 14

"We might have gotten casualties, and the battle ended in the most unusual way possible," said a LavaLiver soldier.

"Well, the battle *might* not be over yet," Obsidian told the soldier, "just because a few thousand Water soldiers got flung a kilometer away doesn't mean that the battle is over."

"Yeah, and I have to agree with Obsidian on this one," General Quartz interjected, "in the Lava-Liver military rulebook, according to section M.239.8B, which is on page 367, states that 'all battles, offensives, operations, etc. must be confirmed as a victory by witnesses deeming that they heard the leader of the opposition say, 'retreat' or all soldiers of the opposition are confirmed dead by a leader of either side. This entire process can be skipped if the alpha and at least three of their five advisors agree. If there are fewer than five advisors active for their alpha, consult section U.234.6A.' So if you were paying attention, I'm pretty sure the leader of the opposition didn't say retreat."

"Uh, I didn't really pay attention because I was kind of falling asleep," one of the soldiers said.

"What?" Quartz asked the soldier. "Do you want to be flung half a mile away like the WaterLivers? I can sure make Obsidian do that."

"Er, no thanks," said Obsidian. "I don't want to fling my own comrades."

"Just as I thought," Quartz scoffed, "anyway, we don't need many soldiers on crossbows. Some of you can even just relax for a little bit. When I mean some, I mean some. I still need some of you to look ahead. Knowing Alpha Atoll and just the WaterLiver military, they're bound to try and come back."

"Do you recall hearing any of the WaterLivers saying 'retreat?'" Solar asked Caracal.

"Nope," said Caracal, "one moment I was hearing battle cries, the clashing of weapons, dying soldiers, and more war-related sounds and the other, I just heard the yelping of soldiers slowly fading away. Of course, I am renowned for having abysmal hearing."

"Wouldn't it be weird if the soldiers were flung by a Pymarto?" Solar wondered.

"That might have actually happened," Caracal replied. "Our own soldiers were also backing up that they saw the Water soldiers being flung a kilometer or two away. Anyway, let's actually hunt."

The two pups split up to open up their chances of finding food. The strategy worked, as Caracal caught three seagulls that were way too far inland, and Solar caught a fawn.

Once they fortunately found each other, Solar and Caracal decided to sit down on the descent of a hill to eat what they got. It was also there that Solar revealed that he traveled to Kloma.

"There's only one continent, and that's Torenta," Caracal countered.

"No, seriously, I went to this other continent. It's called Kloma."

"Is it like under our continent?" Caracal asked.

"If you go through the Northwest Mist and walk for almost four hours, you will be greeted with these small mounds and two large buildings that are called customs," Solar replied.

"Is it also a wolf-dominated continent?"

"No. Instead of wolves, it's owls. They have these things called chiefs instead of alphas. They also have this leader called the Hok, and they're the leader of...you can say the leaders."

"But other than that owl continent–"

"Kloma."

"Other than Kloma, there are no other continents, right?" Caracal asked.

"It's kind of a long story," Solar sighed. "So apparently, we live on this planet called Ğürsa, and on Ğürsa there are five continents: our home continent Torenta, the owl continent Kloma, Petasami, Vetasami, and Pymarto, which is where the Pymartos originated from. And just straight up don't ask why we don't know all this, as that's an even longer story."

"Okay, I won't ask."

Solar and Caracal kept eating for about fifteen minutes. After that, they decided to go back to the Rattlesnake Division camp.

"So, did you guys even manage to get a single bird?" Commander Raven asked them.

"Yeah, three," Caracal replied. "They were seagulls."

"We're in northwestern HillDweller territory," he told Caracal, "there is no way that a seagull ended up this far inland."

"Well, there are three in my stomach right now," she said.

"All right. Did you guys manage to find anything else other than the seagulls?"

"I caught one fawn," Solar informed Raven.

"That's respectable. Anyway, I'm going to need you two to go on lookout duty on top of that hill that's right in front of my tent, and my tent is directly behind us. You're going to switch with Badger and Woodrat in six hours."

"Six hours?!" Solar and Caracal asked simultaneously.

"So what? After these thirty-six hours, you'll be sure glad that I told you guys to go on lookout for six hours instead of nine."

"Solar, it actually won't be that bad," Caracal told him, "one of us could sleep for three hours, and then we switch with each other so that the first one could rest for three hours."

"But then once we switch, the one who scouted first can not only sleep for three hours, but also sleep six more hours since we're switching with Woodrat and Badger," said Solar.

"I mean, I wouldn't mind scouting second," Caracal offered, "I could let you go first–"

"All right, enough," Commander Raven interrupted, "you two, just go to your lookout post. And no resting for six hours!"

The two pups nodded reluctantly and went up the hill for their lookout duties.

The half hour of lookout was uneventful. So were the next fifteen minutes. At the one-hour-and-fifteen minute mark, right as the last speck of the sun left the horizon, Solar noticed small specks of blue coming from the northeast. He assumed that they were WaterLivers and confirmed it two minutes later.

"Uh, Caracal? Remember when I thought that the Waters retreated?" Solar asked her.

"Yes, and I said that Atoll wouldn't give up like that," Caracal replied.

"Turns out you were right," he admitted, "they're coming northeast."

"I don't have good hearing, but I *do* have good eyesight, so let's just see...whoa! They're coming at us! Fast!"

"All right, we need to tell Commander Raven because we need to get our comrades out," Solar told Caracal.

The two pups ran to tell Raven, and he was startled, to say the least.

"Ah, yes, lies, lies, lies," Raven sighed. "I'll just check it anyway."

Commander Raven wasn't expecting much, but when he saw the few thousand WaterLiver soldiers charging east, he immediately changed mood.

"My bad, turns out you were right," he said, "though, for giving me some information, I won't bring you into the battle when I say charge. I'm going to say it right now. All right, Rattlesnakes, to those who are sleeping, wake up! There are Water-Livers out there again. So give it your best and again, I *do not* care if you don't come back. Charge!!"

You could tell that everyone sprang up as soon as they heard that last word, even the DustDwellers that were sleeping. Everyone grabbed their weapons and went into the battlefield. The LavaLivers to their right were a little late when they heard the WaterLivers approaching. Even though neither General Quartz nor Scoria told them to charge, some Lavas went into the continuing battle under Raven.

By the time the last DustDweller entered the battlefield, the Waters were only thirty meters from the Lava and DustDweller camps.

That was when tens of thousands of birds, which were later confirmed to be owls, flew into the battle and were attacking the WaterLivers. The owls looked like ShadowBirds as well as MeadowBirds and Norūeangeans. It took a lot of time for Solar to realize the most crucial part about this surprise attack: these owls were all from Kloma.

Epilogue

Three Days Later...

"Ah, Umbra, done with your scouting already?" the Hok asked.

"Yes, Hok Murk," Umbra replied. "I spent two and a half days there. Also, why did you even send pretty much every single owl to Torenta?"

"As you know, I have the power to look at situations even though I'm not in those situations. And those six wolves, they, in a way, helped secure some peace in Kloma. They were involved in the imprisonment of Chief Veldt, an owl who I just don't like, as well as imprisoning some Norūeangean soldiers, although I don't really get the point of that."

"Okay, so now we're getting lore," said Umbra.

"I'm not done yet. I always get reminders from the spirits when something important happens. During their last day on our continent, a spirit told me that the Stone of Tranquility had been fulfilled."

"Stop giving me lore!" Umbra exclaimed. "Just get straight to the point, Hok Murk."

"Patience, Umbra, patience. A few days later, I was feeling a little bored, so I consulted the Map of Consciousness just to see what they were up to. The brownish-white wolf, the light blue and white wolf, and the mostly blue wolf were in what I believe is a school; the charcoal wolves were in a military division for their tribe, and so was the goldish-gray wolf. When I was focusing on the wolves in the military, I realized that they were going to battle wolves that looked like the mostly blue wolf.

"I was quite confused about why the three wolves were going to battle the tribe of their friend, so I asked the spirits in Daskīmé. About an hour later, one of them told me that the leader of the blue-wolf tribe had declared war on all the other tribes on their continent. Using my retrocognition, I found out that the mostly blue wolf had had a history of not liking the military standpoint her leader has.

"Once I figured that out, it was time to send everybody out to Torenta. The last time I sent most owls to another continent was in Petasami eight decades ago, so it took me a long time to figure out how to send out the message to everyone. I didn't ponder much because I realized that I could just send all of my seventy messengers to spread the word. Next thing you know, tens of thousands of Klomans were going into the Eastern Mist. I hope that answers your question."

"Y-yes, it did, Hok Murk," Umbra stammered, "um, my whole point of coming here was to give you my scouting report. Do you want it?"

"Yes, and as detailed as possible, please."

"The two sides of the battle are still fighting. Even with our Kloman forces, we can't seem to win. For every blue wolf that gets killed, another one shows up out of nowhere. We might need forces from Petasami if we even want to win the battle."

"Really?" Murk questioned. "You have a few thousand wolves and now more than ten thousand owls. How can you lose to a single division of a tribe's military?"

"Correction, it really isn't one big division, there are twenty actual divisions with around 250 soldiers in each of them," Umbra clarified.

"So using my mathematics...there are about 5,000 blue wolf soldiers. So why do you think we need reinforcements?"

"Actually, I don't know," Umbra realized, "but very well. I'm not your advisor, so I'm not going to give you advice."

"Thanks for the report anyway," Murk told Umbra. "Continue scouting with some of the Norūeangeans."

"Thank you," said Umbra.